Zombies, Vamps and Fiends

Ash Hartwell

Edited by: J. Ellington Ashton Press Staff
Cover Art by: David McGlumphy

http://jellingtonashton.com/

"Words have no power to impress the mind without the exquisite horror of their reality"
Edgar Allan Poe

This is for my wife, Nicki.

A Child in Flanders Field

The last wisps of early morning fog still clung to the valley floor as Poppy peered through the battered periscope. Last night's bombardment had left two large smouldering craters, and the dark smoke that now rose from them drifted on the gentle breeze towards her position. It brought with it the bitter, rancid smell present in everything in this godforsaken wasteland. It lingered in the rat-infested trenches and water-filled hollows, it permeated clothing and, if inhaled, felt like it was tearing the lining from your throat.

A sudden gust of wind blew thick black clouds into Poppy's face, causing her to frantically pull at her flimsy face mask as violent spasms wracked her chest. She hunched over as sticky mucus spewed from her mouth and mixed with the blood, piss and shit of a million soldiers who had fought for ownership of this particular piece of blood, piss and shit for the last century.

Wiping her mouth with the filthy sleeve of her coarse, standard-issue tunic, Poppy returned to her lonely vigil. She scanned the enemy's trench out beyond the smoking craters and the rolls of barbed wire designed to tear flesh to shreds, leaving bodies helplessly hanging for scavengers to feed off. It would have been a short sprint on the Academy's flat green playing fields where Poppy had been fastest of the thirteen-year-old girls graduating to combat status in her cadre. But here in Flanders, where the sticky mud sucked you down and German guns showered you with burning lead, those halcyon days on the green and pleasant fields were a lifetime away. So were the German trenches.

"Is anything happening out there, Pops?" The voice came from a small doorway built into a collection of corrugated iron sheets and water-soaked sandbags serving as the company's makeshift billet.

"No. Only movement out there is the damned smoke." Poppy had no need to turn round; the voice belonged to Old Man Josh. Apart from the rats and an infestation of lice, she and Josh were the only living things in the isolated forward command dugout.

"Yeah, I heard you chunking up. You okay?" Josh climbed the

rickety steps onto the wooden walkway and stood next to Poppy. Once there, he began to clean the old sword his grandfather had given him the day he'd left England. In the early days of the war it had belonged to a Polish cavalry officer, and by a complex series of poker games, dead man auctions and theft had ended up in the possession of Josh's grandfather.

"It's nothing that an acute case of death won't cure." Poppy forced a hollow laugh as she surveyed the German trench line through the dirty lens of the periscope. The weak sunlight glinted off something metallic, the brief flash of light the only indication of life from the enemy trench line. "They're watching us too."

"Watching, waiting and dying, that's what this bloody war is all about. Occasional skirmishes and a barbaric slaughter in the pleasant summer months all fitted around hours, days, months of just watching, waiting and dying." Josh's voiced trailed away and, for a moment, he appeared lost in his memories; then he jumped onto the planks running across the bottom of the waterlogged trench. "I'm making a brew, want one?"

Poppy nodded, "At the Academy they preach about how much ground we gain each year, but you know what? It's all bullshit. A few months back I found a map from the failed Versailles peace talks and the front lines are in almost the same place. Over ninety years of killing and we're sat in the same trench our great, great-grandfathers dug."

Josh just gave a resigned shrug as he trudged back into the billet assigned to 5th Live Battalion. Poppy returned to her watching and waiting, her gaze sweeping slowly across the enemy positions as she waited for Old Man Josh to bring the tea. She'd liked Josh from the moment he had taken her and Jude under his protective wing when they'd first arrived at the end of last summer. Even back then he'd been known as Old Man, despite having only just turned eighteen, but then he had called Flanders home for over four long, horrific years.

He was due to return home to England, and a welcome fit for a hero in a few weeks. Josh often talked about his plan to get a job in one of the academies; telling the young draftees thrilling stories of victories won and the glories of war. His greying hair and the haunted look in his eyes told a different story, a story the academies wouldn't want told. But Josh needed a job, and if he towed the line, the academy would look after him.

Josh stepped out of the dilapidated billet carrying two tin mugs filled with a dark brown liquid. "Command finally got round to replacing your friend... What was her name?"

"Jude."

"Yeah, that was it, Jude. Anyway, two replacements are on their

6

way up from the rear. That's if they can find their way." Josh's voice had taken on a sarcastic tone as he'd muttered those last words; it was an undeniable fact that reserve forces rarely made it to the forward command posts. Some would be seconded by other units desperate for extra firepower, however inexperienced they might have been, while others would simply become lost in the warren of trenches, either getting shot sticking their head above the trench top or drowned in the deceptively deep mud.

"Two! We need six to return to full strength. Jude died six weeks ago." Jude had been Poppy's best friend at the academy, yet her voice showed no sign of emotion when she talked about her death. She had long ago learned to accept death as an inevitable consequence of war, and that mourning the dead never brought them back. Not really, not properly.

"We've only been at full strength for about two weeks during the last five years," replied Josh before adding, "And Jude is still officially listed as M.I.A. We don't know for sure she's dead."

"She's dead alright. She became severely shell-shocked; her mind completely unscrewed and she just walked into No Man's Land, looking for her dead mother during an artillery attack." Poppy took a sip of her lukewarm tea. She grimaced, then added, "She's dead, Old Man. No doubt about it."

"We didn't see her go down and neither of us has seen her body since." Josh stared into his tea, aware his false hope wasn't winning Poppy over.

"We'll never find her body. If she was lucky, one of the Kaiser's shells scored a direct hit, scattering her to the wind. Poor Jude's either lost to the Flanders mud or they got her." Poppy nodded towards the sandbags and twisted barbed-wire marking the German trenches. "They would've raped the bits they could and eaten the rest. You've heard what those evil bastards do to prisoners?" She almost spat the words out before falling silent.

"Let's hope she died before they got to her." Josh trailed off into an uncomfortable silence, aware that Poppy wanted the conversation to end. Taking the periscope from her hands, he surveyed the wasteland between him and the enemy lines. After a short while, he spoke again, "The conscripts they send just get younger and younger, especially over the last few years." He sighed, adding, "And they're woefully under-prepared and ill-equipped for frontline conditions."

"Jude wasn't a conscript. Her family had more than enough money to buy her a dodge but she volunteered. She had plans for her life and surviving the Flanders Five was the only way to get the freedom and respect she craved." Poppy coughed hard and spat into the mud before continuing, "She wanted to live her own life and gaining survivor status would have allowed her to do that. Better rations, a house, a job. Without that coveted survivor status, you get so little. What production remains is geared towards the war effort or finds its way into the pockets of corrupt officials."

"That's always been the way," replied Josh. "In the air war in the middle part of the last century, before the fuel started to dry up, my grandfather flew a bomber biplane. He told me that even then resources were shared between arms factories and farms. Those that couldn't work got nothing while the titled and ruling class drove around in yank tanks." Josh took a last swig from his battered mug and, shaking the last drops out onto the ground, continued speaking. "The situation got worse after the oil fires of the 1970's. My grandfather said those wells burned for nearly a decade before they ran dry, the smoke clouds plunged Europe into one long harsh winter that only lifted as we entered the new millennium."

Poppy never tired of hearing Josh's stories and today was no different. She took a sip of her now cold tea before asking, "Did we really drop bombs on Berlin trying to kill the Kaiser?"

"Sure did, but what those government history books don't tell you is that German bombers destroyed large parts of London, including Buckingham Palace." Josh took another look through the periscope, his head moving from side to side as he scanned the wasteland between the two front lines. "I think this particular period of watching and waiting is over and it's time for some dying." He stepped to one side, allowing Poppy to study the German position through the 'scope.

Looking into the eyepiece, Poppy focused on the ridgeline that marked the enemy position. She observed two figures climbing unsteadily from the trench before crawling facedown through the clay-laden mud and under the twisted, rusty barbs of their own defensive barricade. As they scrambled clear of the wire, they slid into a large crater. She could hear distant splashing as the two soldiers floundered in the muddy morass before the natural sucking action pulled them under the waterline.

"I can only see two of them." Poppy quickly searched the trench line before returning her attention to the large crater. A full minute passed before the first figure emerged from the water and began to crawl up the crater's steep, slippery side. The second figure emerged a few moments later and patiently waited its turn to climb from the freezing water. "Their faces are covered in mud, but judging by their movements and the fact they were under the water for so long, I'd say they're Re-Gens." Poppy's speech was slow and deliberate, as if she were weighing up the evidence as she spoke.

"Let me see!" Old Man Josh ordered. Poppy relinquished her position at the periscope and swung her rifle down from her shoulder while Josh inspected the German soldiers advancing on their position. "Oh yeah, Re-Generated for sure. We'll let them get closer then take them down with clean head shots, nice and calm with no dramas, agreed?"

Poppy nodded her acknowledgement as she checked her weapon's magazine, aware there was no margin for error. The only sure way to stop a Re-Gen was by destroying its brain's ability to control the body, and a single shot from distance was the safest, and most effective, way to do this. Once up close, a Re-Gen was ferocious and relentless. Like a trapped wild animal.

One day the dead were just that, dead. Their bodies lost to the quagmire for all eternity, their names inscribed on marble memorials for the living to mourn, their possessions auctioned off by comrades to help the loved ones left behind. The next day, in the long hot summer of 1964, they scrabbled and clawed their way back to the surface intent on continuing the senseless killing. Not in the name of King and Country or the Kaiser, but for their very existence. The burning desire to feast on human flesh drove them on in a relentless assault on the living.

At first the killing was random and indiscriminate. German flesh tasted no different from that of an Englishman or a Frenchman, dark meat no different from white meat. Then scientists discovered that the chemicals they had been using for decades to kill and maim had reacted with the soil and delayed or even prevented tissue death. After that, Re-Generated soldiers became the primary close quarter weapon on both sides of the frontline. They would just keep coming at you, charging fearlessly across No Man's Land. They could be torn apart by machine-gun fire and still advance, intent on the kill.

Poppy ran along the unsteady series of gangplanks that prevented her and Josh from sinking into the quagmire at the bottom of the trench and ducked into a small alcove cut into its side. The niche was protected on three sides by sandbags shored up by criss-crossed planks, supported in turn by thick beams sunk deep into the earth at the foot of the trench wall opposite. She wriggled into a comfortable firing position, laying her rifle on the sandbags in front of her. Staring out through a slit-like opening in the wall of heavy sandbags, she searched the waterlogged wilderness for a sight of the enemy foot soldiers.

"I can't see them," she shouted over her shoulder in the general direction of Josh. Although she raised her voice, it was still calm and controlled. She had engaged the enemy many times before and understood the importance of keeping the emotion and excitement

9

suppressed if she wanted to be an effective soldier.

"They've fallen into another crater thirty yards out. You should be able to pick them off as they climb out." Josh's reply drifted down the trench from his position behind the periscope.

Poppy lifted her rifle and carefully slid the barrel through the oblong gap before pulling the butt tight into her shoulder. Away to her right, a head appeared above the rim of an old crater. Poppy repositioned slightly, bringing her sights into line on the emerging figure. Her slender fingers curled around the rifle's heavy-duty grip. She flexed her trigger finger a few times before gently placing it on the cold steel trigger guard.

Old Man Josh's professional soldier voice broke through her concentration, "Have you got a visual?"

Poppy closed one eye and focused on the figure scrabbling out of the morass in front of her before yelling her by now well-drilled response. "Affirmative!"

"Take it down." Josh's voice was calm, almost matter-of-fact. He had done this hundreds of times and lived to tell the tale.

Poppy took a couple of slow, deep breaths. This was what she had trained for. Ever since she could walk, her guardians at the Academy had taught her to kill. The Germans were responsible for the death of her parents. The Academy had repeatedly told her this, cultivating the seeds of her hatred. Poppy gently squeezed the trigger.

In the distance, the Re-Gen lifted his head as he pulled himself free of the crater. Poppy let her breath out and increased the pressure on the trigger. A loud crack disturbed the quiet morning air and the rifle recoiled into her shoulder. Poppy refocused on the distant figure just as his head shattered in a cloud of powdered bone fragments, leaving the corpse momentarily standing on the lip of the crater. Then it toppled backwards into the mud, its foot twitching as it slid from view.

Josh let out a whooping holler of victory before quickly regaining his professional composure. "Kill confirmed. Second target in view now!"

Poppy concentrated on the second figure as it climbed over its former comrade, intent on obeying its orders to advance, oblivious of the fate awaiting it. She went through her careful preparations again before focusing her sights on the uncovered head of the approaching enemy. Relaxing, she let her finger apply just enough pressure to the trigger.

Nothing happened.

Frantically, Poppy pulled the rifle back from its firing position and worked the bolt back and forth, clearing the chamber before releasing the magazine. The next round had slightly twisted, preventing it from feeding up into the breach. Running her finger along the brass jacket, Poppy gently pushed it down so it could slide back into alignment. She slipped the magazine back into place, using the palm of her hand to push it firmly into its housing before cocking the weapon.

Once more assuming her firing position, Poppy scanned the barren open ground in front of her, following a line from the crater to Josh's observation point. But there was no sign of the enemy Re-Gen.

"For fuck's sake, Pops, shoot it!" Josh's voice sounded unusually panicked. Reacting quickly, Poppy withdrew the rifle from the hole in the sandbags and jumped back onto the gangplank. From further down the trench came two quick muffled pistol shots, then the air filled with a sickening scream which came to an abrupt halt in a wet, coughing choke.

"Josh!" Poppy sprinted along the slippery wooden planks towards the command area. As she arrived in the dug-out, the huge frame of the German soldier stood hunched over Josh's body. It was feasting on the bloodied raw flesh it had ripped from Josh's throat, which was now just a large gaping wound. The sickly metallic smell of fresh blood assailed her nostrils and she fought the urge to gag.

Poppy lifted the rifle to her shoulder and, a little too quickly, pulled the trigger. The shot rang in her ears as the plank on which she stood slid sideways, causing her to fall into the rat-infested pool of slimy, stagnant water beneath the walkway.

Poppy's back slammed into it, the force of the impact driving the air from her lungs and shaking the rifle free of her grip. Her precious weapon sank below the surface as she inhaled, her lungs filling with the rancid liquid. Blinded by the mud, Poppy splashed around helplessly as she tried to clear her airway. With each choking breath she took, Poppy only managed to swallow more of the vile water, until finally, she got a foothold on the muddy trench bottom.

Standing chest deep in the icy pool, Poppy coughed up mouthfuls of watery bile as she wiped the slimy mud from her face. She looked around, searching for the dead German, just in time to see him staggering back to his feet, a large chunk of flesh hanging from his shoulder. Her shot had missed his ugly, grotesque head, but had obviously hit him with enough force to knock him over and prevent him from being able to attack her while she was floundering, defencelessly in the viscous fluid.

Poppy had never been this close to a Re-Gen before. It made her aware of another layer of rotting decay over and above the normal stench that continually lingered in the trenches. As he turned towards her, she could see his dull lifeless eyes set deep into his skeletal features. The greenish-blue skin was pulled tight across his face, the lower half of which had become covered in a macabre mix of Josh's blood and body tissue.

Even after six months of eating rotting food and drinking water infected by putrescent bodies, Poppy's stomach lurched at the sight.

Fighting to swallow the acidic bile surging up into her mouth, Poppy pulled herself through the thick unyielding sludge, dragging herself free of the watery trench floor. She waded towards the doorway of the company billet a few yards away. It was tantalisingly close, yet so far away. Each awkward movement of her arms dragged her deeper into the mire, and all the while she could hear the squelching footsteps of the dead man as he steadily closed the distance between them.

Poppy's outstretched hand touched the wooden walkway surrounding the shabby run-down billet. Her arms ached as, hand over hand, she pulled herself free of the heavy, energy-sapping ooze and onto the rough planks. The foul-smelling warrior from hell was only a few yards behind her, struggling knee-deep through the mire. Summoning all her strength, Poppy got to her feet and staggered through the doorway into the company billet, stumbling exhausted and disorientated towards the pile of rags and equipment that passed as Josh's bunk. She fumbled amongst the torn blankets and damp clothing until her hand found the old sword. Poppy reasoned that as she was still alive and in dire need of a weapon, and Josh wasn't, the ornately engraved blade had become her property. She pulled the polished steel blade free of its scabbard.

The rotting planks behind her creaked as the Re-Gen entered the small living quarters. Spinning round to face her assailant, Poppy lifted the sword out in front of her so the tip of the blade pointed at the dead man's chest. Undeterred and intent on the kill, the rotting corpse kept advancing, driven on by the smell of fresh meat.

Poppy tried to circle to the right, but the man's large frame blocked her and prevented her from being able to escape the compact living quarters. She jabbed the blade's sharp point into the chest of his dirty uniform. The figure now looming over Poppy took a small step back, but showed no sign of pain. She drew the sword back and swung an awkward slash at the horribly lifeless face, but missed by six inches, forcing her to move her feet quickly to regain her balance.

The pungent, putrid smell of the rotting man's flesh filled the room and Poppy could taste it with every gasping, gulp of air she took. The grave-dodging warrior advanced towards her once more, his eyes wide and staring, a side effect of the Re-Generation drug cocktail. Poppy took half a step back and felt the corrugated iron wall press against her back. Aware she could retreat no farther, Poppy felt incredibly small and vulnerable in her oversized uniform. Self-consciously, she tugged at her tunic's sleeve, pulling it up to expose the identification tattoos on her right forearm. The image of whom Poppy believed to be her parents came into her mind. She had never seen her parents, but had always carried this one image locked in her head, taken from an old photograph the academy had shown her. She raised her sword so the blade hovered above her right shoulder.

This was it.

She had not spent six months fighting in this squalid field in Flanders for a cause that no one cared about, for a reason no one could remember, just to die alone at the hands of a deceased German soldier.

Poppy took a confident stride forward, swinging the sword with so much force both her feet lifted from the ground. The blade's tip sliced across the pale, cold cheek of the advancing figure, forcing his head to snap to one side. Stumbling forward, desperately trying to regain her balance, Poppy smashed into the rotting corpse, sending them both to the floor with a heavy thump. She landed on top of her attacker's chest, her face just inches away from his. She arched her back, desperately trying to keep her face away from his ferocious-looking teeth.

The German's emaciated hand clamped hold of her left arm just above the elbow; his deceptively strong grip sent a sharp pain shooting through her bicep. Her right hand still held the sword, but she couldn't swing the blade at the figure sprawled beneath her. Poppy lifted the blade upright into the air and brought the steel handle crashing down into the face of the soldier below her.

Her first blow tore a jagged slice of blackened flesh from the man's cheek, but his fingers maintained their vice-like grip. She lifted her right arm again. This time her powerful downward stroke found its target and the sword's handle embedded in his expressionless left eye. Poppy felt the cracking pop of the eyeball as the entire eye socket crumbled into the man's skull. She kept pushing, forcing the handle deeper. The deceased soldier's grip loosened as he struggled to push the sword from the open cavity she had smashed into his face.

Seizing her opportunity, she rolled off the animated corpse and scrambled to her feet. Taking a firm grip of the weapon with both hands, she raised it above her head and, letting out a loud shriek, swung the blade downwards. The cold steel ripped into the dead figure's neck, sending thick black fluid spraying across Josh's bed.

Placing her foot on the twitching cadaver's shoulder, she tugged the blade free and raised her tired arms for a second strike. This time her savage blow severed the neck completely. The dead man's head rolled away across the floor as the congealed blood and Re-Generation fluid pooled at Poppy's feet.

The only reason she didn't collapse to the floor in exhaustion was the adrenaline coursing through her veins. She stood with her booted feet in the dead man's body fluids, watching as the headless carcass twitched uncontrollably for a brief moment before it finally lay still. Placing the sword on the ground next to her, Poppy unbuttoned her tunic and, shrugging it off her left shoulder, rolled up the sleeve of her scruffy, dirt encrusted shirt and inspected her arm. The skin was already beginning to bruise, but she found no cuts or tears in the skin's surface. She breathed a sigh of relief.

Covering her arm again, Poppy sat alone in the quiet billet. All the others were gone. The children she had trained with; friends she had ridden with into battles both real and imagined; the generation of youth she should have grown old with, were now no more than distant memories. They were taught to believe they were the brightest and best England had to offer, that they would march through the Menin Gate and on to Berlin in one swift, glorious victory. Instead they had all suffered inglorious deaths. A whole generation, just like the countless generations that went before, lost.

She stared at the grime-covered face of the dead Re-Gen, lost in thought. He couldn't have been more than twenty years-old, yet this seemingly eternal war had seen him killed twice.

Then the new trench commander stood up. The professional soldier in Poppy had a job to do, even if she had no men to command. Using both hands to carefully pick up the severed head, she stepped outside. Using her right arm like a medieval trebuchet, she launched the shattered head high over the trench wall and out into the wasteland.

Returning to the billet, she dragged the headless body out onto the gangplank and, struggling under its weight, pulled it into the rubbish disposal area next to the company latrine. She left it there for the huge black rats that swarmed over everything in their relentless search for food. She would burn their leftovers in the weekly waste fire.

Retrieving the sword, Poppy walked back to the body of her fallen comrade. Josh lay with his upper body propped against the wooden slats that prevented the mud walls from sinking back into the trench, his once clear blue eyes staring right through her. Leaning forward, she gently used her thumb and forefinger to close them before standing solemnly, her head bowed.

"I'm so sorry. You were so close to surviving this hellish war and going home to that hero's welcome you always dreamed of." Poppy struggled to keep her voice from cracking. Then, taking a deep breath, she added, "I'm gonna miss you, Old Man."

As she stood in the unnatural silence of the battlefield, a solitary tear rolled down the little girl's cheek, scoring a line through the dirt, before she brushed it away with her blood-stained sleeve. A gentle morning breeze blew through the old trench, taking Poppy's whispered words and scattering them across the graveyard of humanity in which she lived. In which she existed. "I will not break faith with you who have died; you shall sleep forever in Flanders Field."

With that, Poppy took a deep breath, raised the sword, and with one clean blow removed Josh's head from his shoulders. She wasn't going to let them use her friend as a Re-Gen.

Carefully wrapping her comrade's head, she placed it with the fire waste before spending a few minutes at the periscope surveying the ground between her and the German position, ensuring there were no more Re-Gens out there. Once satisfied, she returned to Josh's body and, shooing a couple of rats away that were already gnawing on the exposed neck stump, removed his tattered uniform. Then she began preparing Old Man Josh's body for her supper. Fresh meat was a rare delicacy that she was not going to pass up.

The Serpent's Charm

I stood patiently in the main auditorium of The Raven Club while its esteemed members took their seats amid a low hum of whispered conversations. I checked my pocket watch and noted the appointed hour had arrived; to confirm this, the mighty bell housed high above where I stood began to solemnly strike the hour.

The Bishop of Westminster stepped forward and calmly assumed a position behind the lectern to my left. He'd shed his religious robes for a simple dark suit. At his neck he wore a cravat of the deepest purple, held fast by a gold pin depicting a raven. He raised his hand and the assembled gathering fell silent.

"Dear Lord," the bishop's voice boomed confidently around the auditorium. "We pray thou grant us protection from the horrors revealed in this room, and beseech thee, O' Lord, to give us the strength to fight evil in all its guises, wherever it shall be found. Amen." He nodded to me in the slow solemn way preachers usually reserve for funerals, before taking his seat in the front row.

I surveyed the packed auditorium and noted that the club's members hailed from all walks of life. Nobility rubbed shoulders with commoners, scientists with clerics; even members of the fairer sex were welcome. All were equal within The Raven Club's hallowed walls. Their personal experience of horror beyond the rational experience of mortal men bound them as brothers and sisters.

I cleared my throat and began to recount my tale of fascination. "Ladies and Gentlemen, for those of you who do not know me, my name is Horatio Wolff. I come before you seeking membership of this much revered establishment. I have, as I will endeavour to explain to you, experienced a horror so abominable, so extraordinary, that even now I have trouble believing the nightmares still haunting my sleep." I noticed several of the patrons were gently nodding to themselves, as if they too had suffered the same nocturnal disturbances following their own terrifying experiences.

Taking a few deep breaths to calm my nerves, I began to tell my tale, taking care to choose my words carefully. "I am a man of common valour and even commoner sense. My head is not full of ludicrous notions, nor am I one for flights of fantasy. I believe in the rationality of science, and that, however implausible something may appear, there is always a logical and rational explanation if one cares to find it. However, I must confess these beliefs were shaken by the events I witnessed in the Far East." I'd walked around the lectern and stood not more than three feet from the front row.

"The tale I wish to recount here tonight concerns the darkest and foulest of evils, namely the use of magic far darker than the mere trickery of mortal man in order to destroy a man's soul." I left my words hanging in the hushed chamber and walked back to the lectern, ready to begin my tale. The collective will of the audience for me to continue was almost palpable, the intensity of the atmosphere causing the hairs on the back of my neck to bristle.

"On the death of my father I, being his sole heir, inherited a not inconsiderable sum of money as well as a flourishing spice business. I know some of you here had the pleasure of my father's acquaintance..." Several of the men sat before me nodded, and I recognised most of them as regular visitors to our London home. "Then you will know the diligence he exercised in visiting the company's offices in India and Singapore, and how well-versed he was in the language and customs of the local populations. I, however, had never travelled to either country, and thought that if I were to run the company with the propriety and respect it deserved then I should, and with some haste, make such a journey."

At this point I paused for a moment to take a much-needed sip of water and, I admit, to add a little dramatic effect. A few in the audience took this opportunity to whisper to the people seated next to them, but when I placed the tumbler back on the dark mahogany table and looked up, ready to resume, they fell politely silent.

"I took with me on this trip my dear friend Mr. George Heath-Wilson, whom I had known since our days at school together." I paused to collect my thoughts and prevent emotion from creeping into my voice. "I trusted George and had always found him to be a gentleman of the utmost integrity; indeed, I planned to make him a junior partner and ask him to spend a year in India learning the spice trade business."

"We took a company clipper to the port of Singapore in early spring of this year. On arrival, we sent our luggage on to the hotel while we set off on foot to sample the intoxicating atmosphere of the port's market. I was pleasantly surprised to find all the cultures of the east rubbing shoulders together, from India, the jewel of Queen Victoria's empire, to the Indo-

Chinese peninsula and even as far away as the distant islands of Japan." I was aware that while I was speaking a smile had settled upon my face as I remembered that first care-free day in Singapore, before the horror to come had cast its long shadow over my psyche.

"We strolled among the many street stalls selling ornaments, hand carved from jade and ivory, and clothes of the finest silk embroidery I have ever seen, clothes you would not find in even the finest of London's dressmakers."

"The smells of the food stalls, selling all manner of victuals from across the Orient, mixed with the aromas of the spice traders, conspired together to give a pleasant tanginess to the air. This blended with the thicker, heavier scent of the opium poppy which, I must confess, did help us to preserve a jovial mood, to the extent that the darkness of night caught us unawares." A gentle ripple of laughter spread through the audience, although one or two of the older members looked less than amused.

"Mr. Heath-Wilson and I decided to repair to a small club in the Chinese quarter of the city which, from the outside at least, looked inviting and promised much in the way of sustenance. My companion and I dined well on the most superb cuisine before a waiter escorted us through an arched doorway, elaborately carved with two entwined dragons, into a large room containing a raised central stage. Low tables surrounded by brightly coloured cushions fanned out around the stage, and set further back were several more private booths, each lit by a lavishly carved gas lamp."

I paused as the auditorium's double doors opened to admit a man who was in such a hurry he still wore his long black cloak. He nodded his apologies for the disturbance as the attendant pulled the doors closed and I waited a moment while the newcomer removed his cloak and took his seat.

I raised my voice a little, drawing the crowd's attention back to my story, "We took occupation of one such booth where we sat on large silk cushions. A young woman of Indian appearance, her polished jet-black hair flowing over her shoulders and down to her narrow hips, approached and offered us a cigar — an offer Mr. Heath-Wilson and I were happy to accept. She wore a sari of golden silk that accentuated her natural skin tone and showed off the small ruby situated within her navel. The ruby itself formed the eye of a giant snake tattoo which coiled around her body, the beast's tail looping over her shoulder to curl around the back of her neck. I noticed the young woman had caught the eye of my companion, his gaze following her as she weaved effortlessly between the tables and booths offering the cigars." The room, despite its considerable size, had become quite warm and I needed to take another sip of water to ease my parched throat.

"On the stage, a troupe of seven or eight women danced in time to the beguiling sound of xylophones and several barrel-shaped drums. The elaborate golden headdresses they wore required them to keep their heads still while their bodies whirled in time to the frantic beat. I noticed each of the dancers had fingernails like an eagle's talons. They stretched five inches beyond the tips of their fingers, and between their forefinger and thumb were tiny bells that produced a soft shimmering chime that accompanied the dancer's frenetic movements."

"I now implore you to pay close attention to my words, as the events that occurred next are fundamental in explaining the actions of both myself and Mr. Heath-Wilson. The dancers reached the climax of their intriguing routine and left the stage, to be replaced by a man who must have been not a day less than a hundred years old. He was dark of complexion, his skin standing in stark contrast to the whiteness of his hair, which, although thin in volume, reached midway down his back. A few straggling hairs clung defiantly to his chin to form the remnants of what was once an impressive beard. Save for a cloth of brilliant orange wrapped around his loins, the man was naked." I paused my narrative, aware my next words would shatter the image I had just created in the mind's eye of my captivated audience.

"The old man had begun by sitting cross-legged on the floor then, rolling forward, he pushed his arms down and lifted his body into the air. He then walked around the stage on his hands, soaking up the applause of the crowd, before uncrossing his legs and arching his back so his feet returned to the floor and he slowly pulled his body upright." I looked around the auditorium at the incredulous expressions on my audience's faces before continuing. "This withered old man then lay on what I can only describe as a bed, although it had no mattress. Instead it had a board containing several hundred nails set point upwards, and it was on these the man lay. I swear before God the old man did not once puncture his skin."

Hushed murmurs rippled around the assembled crowd, and I paused briefly before proceeding. "The young woman who'd previously served us cigars appeared on stage carrying a large wicker basket. She placed it in the centre of the stage before handing the old man a long wooden instrument. He sat with it in front of him and began to play the most wonderfully enchanting music."

At this point I hesitated and just stood looking at my feet for a brief moment. If I continued, the good character and reputation of my oldest friend would lie in tatters, a state of affairs that is wholly unfair as he can no longer offer a defence for his actions.

I took a moment to look around the chamber then continued. "The old man then began to play the instrument, his body moving gently with each sweet note. His rhythmic swaying had a captivating charm and I found myself becoming intensely focused on the bulbous end of the wooden instrument. Indeed, so captivated was I that at first I did not notice the giant serpent rising from the depths of the basket."

"The giant beast's broad head swayed in time to the old man's music. Occasionally a long forked tongue flicked out with a barely audible hiss and its neck fanned out forming a giant hood; on the back of this hood were markings which looked like the eyes of a demon."

"It was then, and without any discernible warning, that Mr. Heath-Wilson began to laugh. Then, totally out of character, he began heckling the old man, calling him a charlatan, and I realised, with much embarrassment might I add, that the wine and ambient opium had got the better of my companion's senses. He was struggling to get to his feet, seemingly intent on hurling more abuse at the elderly man, when the snake charmer's assistant enters our booth."

"My companion, who had taken on a character unrecognisable from his normal self, then made an undignified lunge towards her. It was only his intoxication and my quick reactions which prevented him knocking her to the floor. Shocked, I looked back at the stage to see the mighty serpent turning its head in our direction, fixing its dark, lifeless eyes on us. I felt a chill pass through my body which froze me to the core. I sensed I'd just stared into an abyss, and that something had stared back."

"The old man's magical music stopped and the snake abruptly coiled down into the basket, allowing him to replace the lid. He then spoke to the woman in their native tongue. She looked shocked and began trying to argue with him, but he became sharp of tongue and she fell respectfully silent, averting her eyes from his angry glare."

"At this point I became aware that the room had fallen silent with everybody looking in our direction. I had been restraining Mr. Heath-Wilson by holding onto him around his chest, but he'd calmed and so, tentatively, I released my grip. Unsupported, he slumped on the cushions, to the obvious amusement of a few of the locals."

"The young woman had by now recovered her composure; she bowed respectfully to the old man, who still sat on the stage. Then, turning towards my companion and me, she bowed again. Now, Ladies and Gentlemen, I cannot recall the exact wording of our conversations due to the passage of time and the sheer bizarreness of events which have simply defied reason and confused logic, but please indulge my memory."

"She explained in near perfect English that her grandfather was not used to being insulted by a man with the grace of a drunken elephant and the charm of a hog. She went on, that if Mr. Heath-Wilson believed him to be a simple magician who deceived the watchful eye with mere trickery, then maybe he would be so good as to join the old charlatan on stage."

"I must state I was against such an idea, believing it would inevitably result in my companion disgracing himself further. However, he gave me certain assurances to his future conduct and therefore, with reluctance, I agreed to him joining the old man on the stage. The magician's granddaughter led him towards the stage with a sinuous grace, which mesmerised my old friend to the extent that he was unable to divert his gaze above her narrow waist. Even when the old snake charmer greeted him with a toothless grin, my companion's eyes remained focused on the young woman's lithe body."

"She directed Mr. Heath-Wilson to sit on a hastily produced chair. The old man stood before him staring, deeply into his eyes. Then, without warning, he merely snapped his fingers, and Mr. Heath-Wilson's head lolled forward so his chin rested on his chest. The old man turned to the audience and acknowledged the small ripple of applause by raising his hand before requesting our silence. The most extraordinary thing now occurred. The old man pointed a gnarled finger towards Mr. Heath-Wilson, who, in a deep trance, stood up. As the man began to move his finger, Mr. Heath-Wilson started to gyrate and sway as if some inaudible melody gripped his soul, his body bending this way and that, his feet remaining rooted to the stage."

"I must confess that I laughed as heartily as the next person at the sight of such a proper English gentleman swaying like a common drunk, but events then took on a more sinister tone. Mr. Heath-Wilson, with no physical prompting save the dismissive swish of the old man's finger, fell prostrate on the floor, where he began to writhe about in some obvious distress. Then, defying the natural laws of physics, his upper body rose into the air like the body of the snake rising from the basket. His head, swaying back and forth, was face-to-face with the tattooed snake image on the woman's belly, his now open eyes staring transfixed at the jewelled eye of the beast."

I took another sip of water and looked around the packed auditorium. No one took this opportunity to indulge in idle chatter, so I continued. "At this point the old man freed my friend from his trance with another snap of his bony fingers. Mr. Heath-Wilson fell face first onto the floor, much to the amusement of the crowd who cheered heartily, before climbing to his feet, a vexed expression etched on his face. He obviously didn't have a clue about how he'd become the butt of the joke and he didn't like it one bit. He was about to leave the stage when the magician stayed him with an outstretched hand. The young woman translated her grandfather's words, explaining that as he had now experienced life as a snake, then maybe he would have greater respect for those who cared for them. Then the old man disappeared in a cloud of blue smoke, leaving Mr. Heath-Wilson to re-join me in the audience."

"By this point I was in no mood to continue our jovial celebration and persuaded my somewhat confused and angered companion that it was time to leave. We commandeered a rickshaw and gave instruction for it to transport us to our hotel. There, we parted company on less than cordial terms. I believed Mr. Heath-Wilson had behaved with inexcusable rudeness and in a manner unbefitting a gentleman of his status. Furthermore, I believed it would be necessary to re-evaluate my plans regarding his future position within my firm, and I resolved to speak urgently with him in the morning."

"Now, I must tell of an occurrence which I thought little of at the time, but which has since taken on considerable significance. The next morning, after a hearty breakfast, my friend and I went for a short walk and I broached the subject of his behaviour at the club. Mr. Heath-Wilson was apologetic, yet defiant in his stance regarding the old man's validity. He was also preoccupied with lustful and inappropriate thoughts about the snake charmer's granddaughter and so, with a heavy heart, I concluded he was not of the calibre required to represent the company my Father had founded."

"While we talked we strolled past a common street beggar sitting next to a basket not unlike that of the old man, only smaller. Just as we passed him, and, to be honest, paying him little attention, he began to play an identical wooden instrument." The auditorium was silent, engrossed in my account of the incident with the old street beggar.

"As soon as that light, captivating music drifted through the still morning air, Mr. Heath-Wilson began swaying and instantly complained of feeling disorientated and unwell. I naturally helped my friend to bench a few yards farther down the dusty street where, after a couple of minutes' rest, he signalled his willingness to continue our walk and we returned to the hotel without further incident."

"At dinner that evening I noticed Mr. Heath-Wilson had caught the sun and the skin on his forehead had begun to peel. I mentioned this, but he appeared unconcerned, shrugging away any suggestion for him to visit the hotel doctor for some lotion. I didn't push my concern further — he was old enough to know his own mind. However, when we bade each other goodnight on that second day, my companion's temper was shorter than usual. I also noticed on closer inspection that his eyes had become dull and cloudy, as if a translucent skin had been drawn across them."

I lowered my head, struggling to find the correct words to describe the events that followed. Finally I went on, "Ladies and Gentlemen, as I mentioned at the start of this discourse, I am a man who believes in the facts, in what I can see and touch. I have no time for idle ramblings or elaborate gossip, so when I was disturbed in the early hours of the morning by a woman screaming, I naturally assumed she'd discovered a spider or perhaps a mouse in her room. As the screaming continued, reaching the point of hysterics, I thought I should offer my assistance, and, to that end, I left my room in search of the scream's source."

"It did not take me long to find the woman concerned. She was standing in the corridor surrounded by a small group of fellow guests and the hotel's night porter. They were trying to calm the woman, her screams having now given way to a gentle sobbing, it being obvious she had experienced some terror far larger than any mouse. Her complexion was an ashen grey, the blood having drained from her face, while her hands shook in response to the fear still coursing through her veins. Speaking in French, she rambled disjointedly about a giant snake, which, she claimed, had been standing upright in her room when she'd awoken. On hearing this the hotel porter, an elderly man of local extraction, began backing away before turning and running with surprising haste for a man of his years, towards the stairs."

I paused my monologue for a moment to take another sip of water. "I was naturally sceptical of her claim, but did offer to escort her back to her room in search of the culprit. She explained that when she had screamed the snake had run from her room. I must admit I had to stifle a laugh at this point, believing I had misunderstood her French, but she was adamant. The snake had *run* from her room."

"I conducted a brief search of her room and, finding nothing out of the ordinary, decided I needed help if I were to conduct a more thorough search. I knocked with some urgency on Mr. Heath-Wilson's door and, receiving no answer, turned the doorknob. Finding it unlocked, I entered my companion's room. Turning on the gas lamp, I discovered the bedroom to be unoccupied, although the bed was unmade. Lying on top of the rumpled sheets was an empty translucent skin, six feet long, in the shape of a human form."

"I must admit that at that point I had begun to reach a conclusion so terrifying my blood ran cold. I have enough knowledge of serpents to know they shed their skin when they have outgrown it. This, coupled with the peeling skin, the clouded eyes of my companion, and his obvious disappearance gave me cause to believe the unbelievable. Mr. Heath-Wilson had become a snake, or at least snake-like; I could fathom no other explanation."

"As I left the room I encountered the snake charmer and his granddaughter standing in the shadows, their unexpected presence momentarily confusing me. This must have been evident in my expression, as they immediately rushed forward with a little bow. The young woman had on a large hooded cape which partially obscured her face although she made no attempt to remove it when she spoke, explaining that her grandfather was a priest who worshipped Monasa – the snake queen. She continued by saying that he'd been commanded to punish my companion for his conduct towards a Nagi by making him live his life as a serpent, crawling on his belly — a condition befitting his behaviour. She explained it was the snake which controlled the charmer, not the other way around."

At this point I nodded to the man who'd entered the auditorium later than everyone else. He rose from his seat and exited through the chamber's double doors. Once the doors closed, I resumed my tale to the silent audience. "She explained that my companion's predicament saddened them greatly, as the old man had known my father for over forty years and was eagerly awaiting my arrival. He feared Mr. Heath-Wilson's situation would damage the close bond between my father's firm and the Monasa culture."

Unsure of how to continue, I paused and looked around at the assembled members of The Raven Club. Many were acquaintances of my late father, and I was about to reveal facts which he'd taken great pains to keep secret, even from his family. After a brief moment to gather my thoughts, I took a deep breath and carried on with my story. "The young woman went on to quickly explain that my father had embraced the Eastern cultures, especially those of India, and had become a respected member of their community. He understood the way these people lived, their customs, even their beliefs, and acknowledged the importance of the serpent in their culture. He even took a Nagi as his wife."

A hushed whisper rippled around the packed room and the Bishop's face darkened. I was unsure as to the exact reason for this. Was it my father's indiscretion, his bigamous marriage, or the fact he'd abandoned his faith in favour of Monasa that so upset the reserved man of the cloth?

I raised my hand, signalling for silence so that I might go on with my narration, "While she spoke to me in her accented, but perfect English, her grandfather had begun to play his wooden pipe. The soft music floated down the corridor without causing a disturbance to the other still sleeping hotel guests. After a minute or so, a figure emerged from the darkness at the far end of the hallway. It swayed in time to the music as if performing some ancient dance and, as it drew closer, I heard a gentle hissing sound which almost resembled human speech. Then the figure emerged into the light, and for the first time I faced the terrifying reality of what I had previously struggled to comprehend. My friend from those care-free days at school was gone, replaced by the oldest of God's creatures."

A door at the side of the stage opened and the man who'd left the auditorium a few minutes earlier nodded to me from the darkened room beyond. I prepared to deliver the horrific conclusion to my tale of corruption and betrayal. "Ladies and gentlemen, I do not possess the words to describe to you what my friend has become, and so, may I introduce to you Mr. George Heath-Wilson."

Two men carried a large wicker basket onto the stage, placing it in front of the Bishop seated in the middle of the front row. The assembled dignitaries and other members of The Raven Club remained silent, their eyes transfixed by the basket.

"I am afraid Mr. Heath-Wilson has become rather self-conscious about his looks and now needs a little persuasion before venturing out." I turned towards the side door again and raised my arm in greeting. "May I introduce to you Wolff Spice's new Head of Far Eastern Trading, and my half-sister, Nagashree Mishra-Wolff?" A young woman walked confidently onto the stage, her orange sari partially covered by her flowing hooded cape, the serpent tattoo clearly visible on her bare midriff. She smiled at me before offering a little bow towards the audience, after which she began to play the same haunting tune her grandfather had played in that club six months previously.

The music echoed around the auditorium as people craned their necks to get a better view of the basket. Slowly, a scaly human head appeared from its darken recesses. Smooth, rounded shoulders followed, although the arms themselves had disappeared, fusing as one with the beast's body. A long black forked tongue flicked out from the expressionless mouth, sampling the air with a loud hiss which visibly disturbed the watching crowd.

The huge serpent had no ears and the nose was no more than two small holes in the centre of its largely featureless face. When it opened its mouth to reveal a pair of sharp fangs the audience drew back, a few of the women emitting shocked screams. The giant limbless serpent swayed in time to Nagashree's music, the thick muscular body twisting back and forth as it fixed the members of The Raven Club with a sad, cold-eyed stare.

I watched my former friend with detached indifference. I had no time for warm-blooded sentiment; his crass cultural ignorance had been an embarrassment I could not tolerate. Nagashree was a Nagi, the eyes on the back of her cloak mimicking the markings on her hood when she was in her snake form, and he deserved his punishment.

I stepped from the stage confident of my acceptance into The Club's exclusive membership. I doubted anyone present had ever witnessed a more terrifying event than the one they'd viewed this evening. I reflected, for a brief moment, on the possibility that the story foretold of the destruction of my soul, but then the cold-blooded determination returned, banishing such thoughts from my mind.

The Monster in the Fog

Marianne pulled into the driveway of her comfortable suburban home a little after ten. She'd recently returned to work at the local Wal-Mart following the birth of her daughter, Jamie. This had been a hard decision: she desperately wanted to spend more time with her daughter, but the car sales business was going through a significant downturn and Ben, her husband, was no longer able to support the family on his income alone.

Initially finding the challenge offered by motherhood daunting, Marianne had muddled through the first few weeks, learning as she'd gone along. Mostly she missed the freedom she'd enjoyed just a year ago; the parties, her friends. Yes, they'd come round to visit her and little Jamie during the first couple of months, bringing cute little outfits and pink teddy bears, but since then she'd seen little of them. Balancing the demands of family and work gave Marianne precious little time for relaxation and it seemed to her that she'd sacrificed her personal happiness for the sake of everybody else.

After locking up the car, she walked to the solid oak front door. A security light fizzed into life, casting eerie shadows onto an immaculately manicured lawn. Pausing for a moment, she fumbled with her keys looking for the right one. They fell from her fingers, making a barely audible clink on the concrete path. Stamping her foot in frustration, Marianne bent forward, only then noticing the mud splattered up the lower half of both legs. Inspecting the dark marks and clumps of it sticking to the sides and soles of her scruffy training shoes, she tried to remember where she might have gone with so much mud.

As she straightened up, musing that she must have walked through a puddle somewhere, her phone slid from her hand, crashing to the floor before skidding into the carefully arranged flower bed. Retrieving it, she saw with dismay that the display screen had cracked. Tears welled up in the corners of her eyes — that just about encapsulated her life at present.

Carefully wiping away the tears, Marianne walked the last few steps. She entered a dark, silent house, locking the door behind her and sliding the security chain across before tapping her mother's date of birth into the alarm's control panel. Marianne had always possessed a strong fear of someone attacking her while she slept, and was extremely conscientious about home security matters. Satisfied she had safely locked out any threat, Marianne flicked on the main lights.

She was shocked by the sight greeting her.

Ben had left an array of pizza boxes and beer cans on the glass-topped coffee-table. The TV was still on, a paused game menu frozen on the screen. Jamie's toys were strewn across the floor, along with the plastic cup and bowl set Ben's mother had insisted on buying the moment she'd found out Marianne was carrying a girl. The bowl had broken into three bits, as though someone had stood on it.

Marianne surveyed the mess, her hand still poised over the light-switch. She felt the tell-tale burning sensation behind her eyes, her vision blurring as more tears pooled in their corners. Putting her keys into a little glass bowl, she retrieved an old piece of tissue from her pocket and began dabbing her eyes. Then, with a sigh, Marianne began picking up the toys as she walked to the kitchen. Pushing her way through the saloon-style doors, she entered the half-light of the oversized room.

A large pile of washing up covered one side of the granite effect work surface, while the kitchen table was buried under several empty coffee cups, a badly folded newspaper, and a half-sorted pile of clean clothes. More garments were dumped haphazardly on the chairs, while most of the tiled floor was covered with a collection of dirty washing and yet more of Jamie's toys.

Marianne let the toys she'd already collected fall to the ground. Pulling out one of the chairs not covered in clothes, she slumped down onto it. Scanning the room slowly, she let her eyes slide over the chaotic scene, not comprehending what she saw. Only then did she let the tears flow. Rolling relentlessly down her face and neck, they soaked into the collar of her white blouse, leaving wide black streaks down her face where her cheap mascara had run. She sat there for nearly an hour, alone in the glow of the neon down-lighters secreted in the bottom of the kitchen units.

The tears gradually subsided but Marianne made no effort to dry her face. She just remained sitting silently in the half-light, her mascara-smudged eyes staring into the distance, focusing on somewhere a long way outside the walls of her untidy kitchen.

Marianne was no longer looking at the laundry piles or the dirty kitchen utensils. Instead, she watched thick black clouds swirling and spinning around her head, suffocating her in an oppressive fog from which she couldn't or wouldn't escape. The miasma twisted into shapes and faces at once unrecognisable, and yet somehow familiar. It reached out to her, calling her name and, like a child's favoured cuddly toy, gave her security, offering gentle words of comfort, telling her what to do.

Marianne sat in silence, listening.

Eventually she stood up and started tidying the kitchen. As though in a trance, Marianne collected all little Jamie's toys together, placing them lovingly back into the toy box. Pulling a large plastic sack off the roll, she filled it with the discarded pizza boxes and empty beer cans from the main living room, and then used a second bag to clear the rubbish from the kitchen sides. She vacuumed the carpet, even using the thin extension tool to get down the side of the sofa's cushions. Then, gathering all the dirty dishes and kitchen utensils, she filled the dishwasher. Taking a last look around, she stabbed her finger onto the start button.

Once satisfied everything had been cleaned thoroughly, Marianne folded all the clean clothes and placed them in neat stacks on the work surface. Gathering the dirty laundry from the floor, she refilled the large wicker basket then, still standing in the dimly lit kitchen, she took off her shirt and running shoes before removing her denim jeans. Placing the shoes neatly by the back door, she threw her dirty clothes into the basket. Removing her underwear, she slung them on top of her clothes before pushing the basket's lid firmly into place.

Walking naked through the house, Marianne turned off lights as she left each room. Climbing the stairs and walking along the hallway, she felt her feet sink silently into the luxurious deep pile carpet. She paused briefly at the half open bathroom door, and hearing the thin, high pitched tone of Ben's earphones, glanced in. Towels were strewn across the floor. Ben's leg protruded from the bath, his foot resting on the side. Pulling the door quietly shut, she continued on to the end of the hall.

The voices in the fog told her to check Jamie's room, to make sure it was tidy. She couldn't disobey the voices as they would get angry and punish her.

Marianne knew her daughter wouldn't be there. She was at the park. Jamie always loved their little trips there. They would feed the ducks together before sitting on a swing where Marianne would gently swing it back and forth until Jamie fell asleep in her arms. She would be safe at the park. Mothers should keep their children safe.

The voices hadn't wanted her to take Jamie to the park, but Marianne had insisted. "A mother knows best!" She repeated the words out loud, the sound of her own voice startling in the silent house.

Opening the nursery door, she quietly entered the darkened room.

Leaving the door open but not bothering to turn on the light, she started to tidy Jamie's miniature bed. Having straightened the duvet and plumped the pillows she put away the last few toys and turned on the tiny musical night-light. As the soft lullaby played and glowing stars revolve around the room Marianne took one last look before kissing the tips of her fingers, gently blowing it across the room. Finally, she pulled the door shut.

It was getting late now and Marianne needed to get Ben to bed. He always got so grouchy when he didn't get enough sleep. Walking back to the bathroom, she pushed the door open and stood naked, hands on hips, in the doorway, the bright fluorescent lights making her pale skin shine with a dazzling brilliance.

Ben didn't acknowledge her arrival. Lying face up in the reddish brown water, he stared at the ceiling.

Marianne didn't expect him to move; in fact it would've surprised her if he had. Particularly following the savage blow she'd dealt to the back of his head with a crowbar. After that it had just been a matter of pushing his shoulders down so his face was completely under water.

It had taken nearly two minutes for her husband to drown. The voices had cheered her on, willed her to succeed. The first thirty seconds had been easy. His face slipped gently under the water, his head wound spilling bright red blood into the warm bath-water. But, driven by the primal urge to survive, his damaged brain had begun to panic as it had desperately struggled against the effects of oxygen starvation. His wildly kicking legs and flailing arms had churned the water into a pink foam, sending it cascading over the rim of the bath and making the floor slippery, where it had prevented her from getting a firm grip, hampering her efforts.

Finally, he'd stopped struggling. His body had fallen limp, a final bubble escaping his blue-tinged lips before bursting at the water's surface. But Marianne had kept pushing downward, counting to ten slowly in her head. His lifeless, accusatory eyes stared up at her from beneath the water, eyes that bored directly into her soul, to the monster lurking there.

The fog had billowed in then. The reassuring voices had told her she'd done the right thing; that he had deserved to die for the things he'd done to her. It had fully consumed her, swallowing her up and leaving her stranded in the black void at its centre. She remembered the argument about Jamie, the words swirling about in the fog, but nothing else since she'd pulled into the drive almost two hours ago with muddy shoes.

Marianne calmly reached down into the bloody water and pulled the bath plug free. The dirty brown water immediately began to gurgle away, gradually revealing more of her husband's corpse. She removed his headphones and turned off the music. He'd always enjoyed listening to music while taking a bath, but tonight she'd put one of her playlists, the one he'd hated most, on repeat.

It took Marianne several minutes of slipping and sliding to pull Ben's dead weight over the edge of the bath and drag him from the bathroom and across the hall into the bedroom. After another few minutes of struggling, she managed to manhandle him onto the bed, their naked flesh rubbing together for the last time as she stood up.

Marianne laid Ben's head on his pillow, a large pinkish stain forming as the mixture of blood and water in his hair soaked into the pillow-case. She stood there looking down at him, a pink halo gently creeping out across the crisp white linen. Marianne thought that he finally looked calm and peaceful. He'd been so angry recently; he'd kept telling her that she needed help, telling her that she wasn't fit to be a mother.

It was just after the birth of Jamie that Marianne had first experienced the fog. At first it was a mere fleeting wisp of mist, so fine she'd barely noticed its presence. Then, as Ben had grown angrier and Marianne had remained cooped up at home with only Jamie for company, the fog had grown thicker, surrounding her like a blanket. It was her little area of tranquillity, free from the stresses of life. After a while the voices had started speaking to her: quiet and distant at first, but offering comfort and understanding. They understood how she was feeling, telling her she wasn't ill, that she shouldn't listen to Ben. What did he know anyway? She was Jamie's mother and it was her responsibility to look after her. Not his. Not his bloody interfering mother's, and certainly not some interfering social worker.

After a while the fog had become darker, thicker, the voices more sinister. They had whispered to her, telling her to teach him a lesson. At first she thought they'd meant she should leave him, go stay with her mother for a while so he learnt to appreciate her, appreciate what he had. Only when the fog had cleared one day, its laughter echoing quietly inside her head, and she'd found herself sitting on the ledge of a high-rise, did she realise what the voices had really meant, what they were truly after.

Marianne had stood alone in the oppressive mist, attempting to reason with the faceless voices, arguing with them, even trying to lie to them. But they always knew the truth, punishing her for each little indiscretion. Just recently, when the fog had drifted away leaving her alone with her thoughts, she'd noticed deep cuts on her arms and legs.

Bending over his lifeless form, Marianne gave her husband one last kiss, then pulled the sheet over his face. She turned and walked purposefully back into the bathroom. Standing naked in front of the full-length mirror, her smudged black eyes looking back at her from her

31

mascara-streaked face, Marianne saw nothing apart from the monster raging inside.

She'd always been so careful with locking the door, so careful not to let a monster in. But the monster had been there all along. Biding its time, it had remained hidden in the mist; it had crept up on her unnoticed, stalking her with a malign determination.

And now Marianne stood, stripped bare before it. Looking back at her was a familiar stranger.

The monster had taken her family while she'd stood helplessly by and watched. It had destroyed her life from the inside; a rotten apple in a barrel of the plumpest, juiciest fruits. It had turned the gentle flame of her soul into a raging inferno, threatening all in its path, and only she could extinguish it. Only she could destroy the monster inside.

Reaching out with a shaky hand, Marianne picked up the razor from the edge of the custom-made sink. The fog became heavy black clouds filling the whole room, yet Marianne could clearly see the monster smiling at her. It was willing her on, throwing down a gauntlet to see if she'd accepted its challenge. Daring her.

Her first cut was a slow downward slash from the base of her throat and down between her breasts, stopping just above her belly button. A thin red line appeared on her pale skin, like an artist's first tentative brush-stroke on a new canvas. The line slowly thickened, drops of ruby red blood slid down her body and dripped on to the floor.

The monster screamed with joy.

Marianne doubled over, the agonising pain exploding along the path of the razor. The cut widened and blood gushed from the gaping edges of the wound. It flowed down her legs, joining the smaller droplets on the floor, mixing with the spilled bathwater to form little flower-like swirls.

Straightening herself up, one hand gripping the edge of the sink, Marianne looked deep into the monster's black-stained eyes, then swiftly drew the blade across her throat.

The monster choked.

Marianne smiled as she watched the blood-spray arcing across the mirror, before her legs gave way and she sank to the floor. In those few precious seconds before her life drained away across the bathroom floor, Marianne saw that the fog had finally lifted, and the monster inside had gone.

A New Lease of Death

Thumbing the tiny lock symbol on his key, Howard headed for the arena. He'd been driving for several hours but the sun's weak autumnal rays were still only just appearing above the horizon. He desperately needed bacon and caffeine, as well as to relieve the pressure on his bladder; his precious cargo could wait for ten minutes. Besides, he wanted to check out the venue and ensure that everything was as it should be.

Having emptied his bulging bladder and consumed a greasy bacon sandwich from one of the catering vans scattered around outside the arena, he headed for the backstage storage area. Walking along the rows of small cubicles fitted with high tensile steel cages, he nodded to a few people he recognised from his fifteen years on the circuit. Before long he found the cubicle with his name printed on a piece of paper pinned to the wall. The usual registration sheets and insurance paperwork lay on the one plastic chair provided.

Howard gave the cage a firm shake, checking the door catch and locking mechanism before taking the paperwork to the registration desk at the main show ring's entrance. Sharing a joke with the administrator, he signed the registration sheets, paid the entrance fees and returned to his truck in the competitor's secure car park.

The specially enclosed area was slowly filling up as Howard began checking his precious beauties. Temporarily erected steel perimeter fencing with a ten yard wide strip designated 'No Parking' allowed security personnel a clear sight of the fence-line surrounding the car park. This was standard procedure at every event, but Howard and his fellow competitors were at ease with the need for such high security levels. After all, the contents of his truck would command a high price on the black market.

Howard cut the plastic security tag and pulled the thick chain out of the looped door handles. Tugging hard on them, he swung both doors open before securing them against the side of the truck.

Three figures stared back at Howard, shielding their eyes against the early morning sunlight. As they attempted to stand on unsteady legs, a series of low wheezing groans filled the truck's cargo area, punctuated by occasional hollow thumps as travel-weary bodies stumbled into the trucks' steel inner walls.

Howard climbed into the back of the vehicle, quickly checking each individual cage to satisfy himself the locks were still sealed. "Shush. I'll sort out your breakfast in a minute." Completing his inspection, he moved through to the back of the trailer unit where an old fridge stood and removed three plastic bags each about the size of his forearm, along with three bottles of water. Returning to the cages, Howard twisted off the bottle caps, setting them down next to each cage before taking a small bunch of keys from his pocket.

Unlocking the first gate, he emptied one of the bags onto the floor, the raw meat sliding from the upturned bag with a soft, wet splash. Howard quickly placed a bottle of water inside the cage before pulling the gate shut. As he did so, the cage's inmate swooped forward and began tearing frantically at the meat, devouring each torn strip in a matter of seconds. Howard swiftly moved between each enclosure repeating the feeding process. It was important they all ate together, the meat presented to them in turn effectively enforcing their pack hierarchy.

Pulling down the hydraulic loading ramp, Howard sat and waited for his wife to arrive. Geraldine had stayed behind to feed their other stock before collecting their assistant, Jess. As the law prevented him from unloading until he had the required one-to-one ratio, all he could do was sit and wait while listening to the feeding frenzy.

The early morning sun was just beginning to warm his face when he saw his wife's car pull into the competitor's car park. Getting to his feet, he waved as she carefully wove through the now busy car park. "Hi. All fed and watered and ready to go," Howard said as she parked up next to his truck.

"Hi. Let Jess and I get this stuff inside, then we'll take them in," she replied, giving him a quick hug before walking up the ramp into the back of the truck. A loud commotion greeted her arrival and the vehicle began rocking on its suspension, "How are my babies this morning? Mummy's going to unload your gear, then she'll be back to let you out."

As she and Jess carried the equipment away across the car park, a series of small throaty moans came from inside the truck. Smiling, Howard said, "She'll be back in a minute." They all loved Geraldine, she had a way with them no one else did.

Approaching a cage Howard spoke firmly, "Hands!" The figure pushed her hands through a slot, enabling Howard to bind the wrists with nylon cuffs. He never liked doing this but, when in public areas, it was a necessary evil. The consequences of a zombie running amok in a crowded car park, street or shopping mall were just too horrific to consider, especially after that incident in a school in Amsterdam. By the time Geraldine and Jess had returned, all three zombies had been secured and were jumping about excitedly. They knew it was getting close to show time.

The first to be unloaded was Brianna, a purebred Californian Spoilt. Competing in the Young Adult class, she'd performed consistently well since Geraldine had persuaded Howard to import her almost eighteen months ago following her drug-induced heart failure. Stroking Brianna's long, bleached blond hair, Jess said, "Let's go and brush that for you." Giving a little nod and a half smile, Brianna allowed Jess to lead her towards the arena's iron gates.

Next to leave the gloom of the trailer and step into the now bright sunlight was Howard's oldest zombie, an English Aristocrat named Pendragon. He competed as an Un-worked Leisure (Retired) and had, in his long distinguished career, won many competitions in both Prime and Senior classes before graduating to the Retired category. Howard had showed Pendragon at the highest level and, with him, had won the highest award offered by the United Nations Department for Expired And Dead Humans, (or Undead H as it had become known). The small gold statue presented for 'Outstanding Achievement in Zombie Care' took pride of place in Howard's bulging trophy case.

As Howard led the zombified aristocrat away, Geraldine started unloading the last one they were due to show. Rhoderick, a squat muscular exhibit, was a Welsh Miner by breed, just as his father and grandfather before him, with his mother being the daughter of the village vicar whose parish included the old coal mine. Competing in the Labouring Prime class, he possessed a fiery character, with a tendency to be aggressive towards other contestants, and on odd occasions, judges he thought were being rude.

Rhoderick bounded off towards the entrance dragging Geraldine behind him. He loved the show environment, often spending most of the day jumping around excitedly, usually having to spend much of the time he wasn't in the show ring secured in a holding cage. Geraldine apologised to the security guard on the gate as Rhoderick tried a little too enthusiastically to hug him. Luckily, the guard thought the incident amusing and didn't feel threatened by Rhoderick's big toothy grin.

Having safety transported all three ex-humans to the tiny cubicle, Howard's team could begin the hard work of preparing them for the day's competition. The first due to be shown was Brianna, so Howard secured the two males in the holding cage. Pendragon stood with a regal, faraway look in his eyes while Rhoderick jumped around trying to reach through the bars to anyone walking past.

Jess set to work dressing and grooming Brianna. Removing the loose fitted jog top Brianna always wore travelling to shows, she, with Geraldine's help, got a bra on to Brianna's surgically enhanced breasts. She came from one of the few breeds allowing such changes, provided the surgery took place pre-mortem.

Brianna had hated underwear in life and still always put up a struggle. Jess stroked her shoulder reassuringly, "It's alright Bree, it's not going to hurt you, and you always look so beautiful dressed up." Letting out a low moan, Brianna put her head on Jess's shoulder. Laughing, Jess helped her sit down, "You're going to wear the blue today, it so matches those beautiful eyes of yours." Bending forward, as if sharing a girly secret, she added. "And, just maybe, that gorgeous young man you saw last month will be here today." Smiling, Brianna let out a staccato rasp that in life would've been a girly giggle.

Jess rubbed preserving lotion into the dead woman's skin, paying particular attention to dry areas around the mouth and neck, before gradually working down her back, chest and arms. After a short while Geraldine took over, removing Brianna's baggy sweat pants and applying the greasy lotion to her legs, allowing Jess to style the long blond hair which was so typical of the breed.

The hair was becoming increasingly dry and Jess needed more and more lotion to make it manageable. Finally, after almost an hour of teasing and primping, Brianna's hair had the desired flowing curls of the 1970's retro style. Everybody did the J.J from Criminal Minds or a Jennifer Anniston look, whereas Geraldine wanted something more Farah Fawcett. As soon as she finished with the hair, Jess began applying the make-up's base foundation, carefully covering the uneven blue and green hues to produce a blemish-free, healthy skin tone. Geraldine would finish the job by applying a glittery blue eye shadow and a subtle, but concealing lipstick just before show time.

While his wife and Jess worked, Howard cleverly appointed himself *tea boy* and went off in search of refreshment. The zombies loved coffee, but Howard only allowed them the caffeine-charged drink on show days as they had a tendency to become overexcited on it. However, it did put a glint in their eye and a spring in their step, serving them well in the ring. The trip also allowed Howard time to check on the opposition and touch base with a few fellow show breeders – a term so much better than Corporeal Harvester or Body Farmer.

This particular show had become the region's most popular event, with success leading to national or even international recognition. It also had a special place in Howard's heart as it had been the first major show he'd won, and while out celebrating his triumph, he'd met Geraldine. The other contestants viewed them as the people to beat, but that didn't stop Howard from considering a few of them friends. Weaving his way through the crowds, shaking hands and exchanging pleasantries, Howard was at his happiest, a benevolent king among his adoring subjects, although he was aware of plots to overthrow him and seize the crown.

Howard browsed a few of the dealer stalls which displayed products from exercise chains and travel cages, to nail polish, shampoo and preservation cream – a mix of embalming fluid, moisturising cream and a synthetic copy of an enzyme found in the giant turtles of the Galapagos Islands. At one stall he bought an evening wear shirt for Pendragon which came impregnated with odour control chemicals, as powerful spotlights used in main display rings often caused small areas of decomposition during shows and smelly exhibits lost marks.

He was just buying a large bag of dried pig brain training treats when he heard the distinctive voice of his oldest friend and fiercest rival, Charles. "Well hello, Howard." He turned to see Charles's domineering frame as it strode towards him.

"Charles, how great to see you," the two men shook hands warmly. Looking at his friend quizzically, Howard asked, "How are you keeping? We've been meaning to come and visit you, but with the show season in full swing..." He let his words trail away, only too aware how inadequate his excuse sounded.

"That's all right, I understand. I'm doing okay, some days are worse than others, but that's to be expected." Charles took a deep breath before continuing, "Since Sara's death I've decided to retire. She always wanted to be a show zom, would've been one of the best too, but due to the nature of her death it wasn't possible to..." Charles's voice cracked into a whimpering sob.

Reaching out a comforting arm, Howard led his friend towards a nearby refreshment stall. Buying two coffees, he placed one in front of Charles who, having regained his composure, was busy checking his phone messages. Looking sheepish, Charles apologised and thanked Howard, raising his coffee cup in a mock toast before adding, "What would Sara say if she could see me now?"

The two men sat looking at each other for a brief moment before saying in unison, "Shut up! You cry like a bloody hormonal girl." They burst out laughing at their shared joke, the awkward tension of the last few minutes forgotten.

It took a little time for the old friends to stop giggling. Wiping the tears from the corner of his eyes, Howard was finally able to ask, "What's happening to your stock? I'm guessing the older ones will decomp in peace on your farm, but you've got some quality youngsters in that group."

Taking a sip of coffee from the take-away cup before placing it on the table, Charles looked at Howard, a huge grin threatening to split his face in two. "I've sold the lot to a Chinese collector. He offered almost twice my own valuation and I couldn't sign the contract quick enough." Again the two men shared in the laughter. They'd first met at a novice show, each of them owning one scraggy second-hand zombie, and in a world that could be so petty and spiteful their enduring friendship was a refreshing change.

"That's the way of it; it's becoming a rich man's sport; all the money is moving east." Howard spoke with experience, he'd attended a competition in Hong Kong and it was a glitzy, gala affair with television coverage, a world away from the home or European circuits. "I expect there's a lot of interest in Western exhibits and that would interest the advertising people and big sponsors."

"I expect so, but for me it's time to cash out. I'm too old for this shit now; the new rules and regulations, finding suitable corpses. It's not like the old days when you could enter road kill and win. My only regret is never winning one of those shiny gold statues."

Howard sat nodding his head in silent agreement as his friend spoke. When Charles finished speaking the two men spent a short while in reflective silence before Howard said, "I'll miss you, my friend." He raised his cup and downed the last of his coffee before getting to his feet, "I'd better get back, otherwise Geraldine will feed my brains to the zoms tonight."

Charles smiled, a faraway look in his eyes, "I'll be over to see you once I've done my last performance. I need to say my goodbyes and tie up a few loose ends." The two men shook hands and Charles, walked briskly into the gathering crowds, leaving Howard to purchase more coffee before returning to the preparation area.

Having finished getting Brianna ready, Geraldine and Jess had turned their attention to Rhoderick. Jess was trying to comb the remains of breakfast from his beard while Geraldine sprayed softening lotion on his wiry hair. They'd already dressed him in his leather trousers and work boots, his first demonstration being about raw power and strength. The costume for his second demonstration was hanging on a rail next to Pendragon's smart business suit.

As Howard returned he smiled at Brianna, giving her a wink. She responded by clapping her hands and rocking from one foot to the other. Going to a small table, he set down the two cardboard carriers loaded with takeaway coffees. He removed a skinny latte and handed it through the bars to Brianna, who immediately began drinking, oblivious to the heat of the recently boiled milk. Speaking to the two women wrestling with Rhoderick's hair, he vaguely gestured towards the drinks. "I'll leave yours here. His choco-mocha is here too." He was rewarded by one of Rhoderick's toothiest grins.

Picking up an espresso he handed it to Pendragon, who sedately sipped the hot black fluid like the upper class gent he had been in life. Leaving the ageing zombie to finish his drink, Howard took a gulp of his third coffee of the morning, knowing he'd regret it later. He could already feel the pressure building in his bladder, and at his age the valves and pumps didn't always work as they once did. Removing the new shirt from its cellophane wrapping, he held it up for Pendragon's approval. Pendragon feigned disdain at having to wear something off-the-peg.

Laughing, Howard collected the suit from the rail before opening the cage to let him out. Stepping back, he signalled the walking corpse through the gate. But Pendragon remained rooted to the spot. He was still holding the tiny cardboard cup, staring at it with a mixture of confusion and fascination. Stepping into the doorway and gently reaching out his arm, Howard nudged the zombie's shoulder, asking, "Pendragon, are you coming?"

The elderly corpse looked up and, as if seeing Howard for the first time, started walking out of the cage, his gait slow and unsure. Stepping out of the way, Howard noticed Pendragon stumble slightly; the cup fell from his fingers, the remains of the coffee splashing across the concrete floor, leaving Pendragon flexing his hand incredulously, his gaze switching between his hand and the pool of coffee. "I'm not sure you're up to performing today," suggested Howard. "Maybe we should rest you today and give you a medical inspection when we get home?"

Letting out a sharp angry moan, Pendragon snatched the suit from Howard's hand and, to prove his point, started tap dancing. His previously cumbersome feet flew nimbly through the intricate routine. "I don't think he agrees with you," said Geraldine, applauding Pendragon's impromptu performance.

"Okay, okay. You can perform," said Howard, holding his hands up in a gesture of surrender. Smiling in the awkward, slightly disturbing way only zombies can, Pendragon bowed theatrically, milking the applause his performance received from some of the surrounding stalls. Removing the comfortable sweatshirt Pendragon had travelled in, Howard noticed it was damp to the touch; unusual, as zombies didn't sweat. Pulling the heavy cotton free of the man's arms he inspected the flesh on his back. It was also damp and in places small droplets of pale yellow fluid oozed from open wounds. The pungent smell of necrotic tissue filled the air. Even Howard, a seasoned veteran in zombie care, flinched as the stench of rotting and decaying flesh assaulted his nostrils.

"Geraldine, could you give me a hand to patch these holes? Hopefully we've caught this in time, but it's going to need opening and packing tomorrow." Howard put a brave face on for the benefit of the zoms. They didn't understand full speech anymore, just a few commands and their names, but they were adept at interpreting vocal tone and facial expressions. Howard didn't want them picking up on his uncertainties.

Together, he and Geraldine attempted to suture the wounds, but the soggy flesh just tore as the thread pulled tight. They packed them as best they could and covered each wound with a large self-adhesive dressing. Once satisfied, Howard began to dress Pendragon, sensing that it might be for the last time.

Once Pendragon was resplendent in his new shirt, silk tie and one of Howard's old Armani suits, complete with matching tiepin and cuff-links, he escorted Howard to the competitors' viewing area to watch Brianna perform. As soon as her entrance music filled the auditorium, he began clapping enthusiastically. Pendragon had become infatuated with the petite Brianna the moment she'd arrived from Los Angeles dressed in a pink designer track-suit, her hair pulled away from her face and held in place by the expensive sunglasses perched nonchalantly on top of her head.

Brianna strode confidently into the ring. Walking purposefully towards the judges' table, she stopped, striking a pose. Howard knew she would be staring directly into the eyes of one of the judges, almost daring him to take marks away. Then, with a swirl of blue dress, she turned away from them, striding towards the centre of the arena where she stopped to perform a series of ballet-style movements demonstrating her strength and control. After a few minutes, Jess ran from the edge of the arena and balanced a book on Brianna's head. She immediately began walking sedately back to the judges. Having paused for a few seconds to prove the book was still under control, she flicked her head, catching the book one-handed before running from the arena waving and blowing kisses to the cheering crowd.

The pressure was now on Jess. The rules stipulated a turnaround time of less than two minutes. During this time she needed to change Brianna's costume and lay out any props needed for the more physically demanding section of the competition. Howard was fond of saying that the changeover period sorted the serious contenders from the serial offenders, as marks were lost for time faults and dress faults. That was why Brianna's second costume was a simple affair of a blue bikini top and cut off denim jeans. It was almost the national dress of her native Californian beach and allowed the judges to see her extraordinary physique while she performed. Jess spent several hours a day putting Brianna through her paces in the weight room or on the treadmill. Today Brianna was performing tricks on a skateboard, followed by a short dance routine even Jess thought a little risqué, and she had been the choreographer.

Completing her routine, Brianna lay sprawled on the ground right in front of the judges. As the last few beats of music echoed around the arena there was a brief awkward moment of silence before the crowd rose to applaud. Looking away to his right, Howard saw Jess punch the air in delight, then sprint into the ring to reward Brianna.

Leading Pendragon away, Howard hurried to congratulate Jess and Brianna on their performance. The announcer started reading out Brianna's scores, but the roar from the crowd drowned him out and Howard had to stop and look up at the scoreboard. Three perfect 10's and two 9.5's. He would struggle to keep Jess much longer as she was already making a name for herself as one of the country's leading trainers.

During the brief lunch break following Brianna's class, which she won by a mile, Howard celebrated with Jess and Geraldine before returning to the viewing area to watch Charles parade his entire stable to the crowd. It was his final farewell to the sport that had become his life. As he left the arena the emotion became too much and tears rolled down his face. His zombies formed a guard of honour, each bowing in turn as he passed.

Immediately after lunch it was Pendragon's chance to perform. Standing at the arena entrance, Howard gave the zom a final pat on the back as his chosen music started. Walking confidently out into the centre of the arena he had commanded for so many years, he politely nodded to the crowd, touching the brim of his bowler hat as he did so. He paused for a moment; then, like a member of the Queen's guard, he shouldered arms with his umbrella before strolling towards the judges using the umbrella as a walking stick. Stopping in front of them, he twirled the umbrella before turning to walk away.

As Pendragon completed the turn, he stumbled. An audible gasp rose from the auditorium as the ageing zombie's legs fold under him and he sank to the floor. Rushing to the stricken Pendragon's aid, Howard immediately noticed his leg was twisted at a bizarre and grotesque angle, the sharp jagged end of the snapped femur protruding through a tear in his trousers. The unmistakable stench of putrefied flesh filled the air, becoming stronger with each passing second as the decomposition gasses leaked from the open wound.

Kneeling next to Pendragon's prone form, Howard assessed the injury and inspected the protruding bone. The geriatric zombie lay still as his master manipulated his leg, the occasional groan the only sign he was unhappy. As zombies didn't experience pain to the same levels as living humans do, Howard was unconcerned by the moaning. More worrying to him, however, were the tears in the expensive suit's material which increased the exposure of subdermal tissue to air. This would cause the leg to enter Rapid Decomposing Activity, or RDA, which would spread throughout Pendragon's body within a few hours.

To the living dead, RDA is fatal. It causes the victim's carefully preserved cadaver to liquefy from within, while they remained conscious, until the disease reached their brain. Then they became confused and volatile, often entering aggressive rages, until the brain decomposed sufficiently for them to slip into a state similar to a coma and then die. All this could happen within three hours at least, but rarely more than six.

A couple of safety marshals joined Howard in the centre of the arena. Standing up, he greeted them with a brief nod, whispering to the first, "It's a bad break, get the ZMT." As the man moved away to radio for assistance, Howard sat down next to Pendragon. Knowing the rules governing RDA (he had advised the United Nations in his role as Ambassador for Zombie Rights), he was aware he would have to put emotion to one side.

For Pendragon, there would only be one outcome.

Smiling down at his faithful old friend who'd allowed him the honour of riding with him to the pinnacle of their sport, Howard felt his heart would break. Gently rubbing Pendragon's shoulder, he became aware, almost for the first time, that the flesh under the thin shirt and jacket was cold. The safety marshals hurried away, mumbling something about finding some screens, passing the ZMT as she ran towards the stricken Pendragon.

Without even looking at Howard, the ZMT said, "Hi, I'm Carol. What's the problem?"

"Fracture to the left leg," Howard said, a tone of mild irritation in his voice as he pointed to the obviously misshapen limb. Then, ignoring the fresh-faced woman's glare, he added, "He's now going into RDA." Saying the words out loud caused tears to form in the corner of Howard's eyes as he fought back the surge of emotion that threatened to overwhelm him.

"Let me be the judge of that!" Carol spoke with the confident air of a professional who didn't appreciate amateurs trying to do her job. Bending to inspect the leg, she inhaled the distinct stench of putrefaction, screwing her face up involuntarily. Barely even pausing to look at the injured leg, the young ZMT stood up, seeking fresh, clean-smelling air to breathe. "I agree, that's definitely RDA, and, judging by the odour, it's already quite advanced."

Howard nodded in silent agreement, detached from the events unfolding around him. He was unaware that Carol was speaking to him until she reassuringly touched his arm. "Hey, you okay? He hasn't bit you or anything?" Howard just shook his head as she continued, "We're going to have to destroy it now." Her fleeting moment of concern was now buried under a dour professional countenance.

"His name is Pendragon," Howard whispers.

"What?" Carol was fumbling around in her large luminous backpack, not looking at Howard.

Raising his voice, no longer able to disguise his anger, he repeated himself. "I said his name is Pendragon!"

Looking up sheepishly, Carol muttered an apology before producing a box of syringes from her backpack. Removing one, she tore it from its sterile wrapper and pushed a needle taken from a second box onto its end. Returning her attention to her rucksack, she pulled out a bright yellow canister containing two glass vials. She removed a green one before snapping its top off to draw fluid into the syringe, then repeated the process with a red vial, allowing the two drugs to mix.

"I took him to the United Nations a few years ago, you know. The best zombie I ever saw perform. On his day he could beat the world without breaking a sweat..." Realising the irony of his words, Howard trailed off into a soft, nervous laugh. "Not that sweating is popular among zombies, of course."

"Are you ready?" Carol was poised, syringe in hand, aware of the urgency of the situation.

Howard reached for Pendragon's cold hand, nodding. Tears rolled freely down his cheeks as he looked into the old man's eyes. The green contact lenses stared back at him as Carol administered the mixture of drugs, neutralising the synaptic enhancers used to keep Pendragon's nervous system working. Howard felt a slight, almost imperceptible squeezing on his hand before Pendragon's head rolled gently onto its side and he was gone.

Returned to the dead where he belonged.

Patting the corpse's shoulder one last time, Howard whispered a final farewell before standing and walking across the now-hushed arena. A quiet ripple of applause began spreading around the stadium, steadily growing to a climax as the shocked audience rose to their feet.

Overwhelmed, Howard managed to give a small bow in

acknowledgment before stepping into the tunnel.

Howard was greeted by Geraldine, the two of them collapsing into a sobbing embrace. Jess was holding Brianna's arm, preventing her from running into the arena in search of her beloved Pendragon. After a short while the curtains parted and the marshals entered, rolling a gurney with a sheet-covered figure strapped to it.

"I'm sorry," Carol said, following the two men, "but I need you to sign the release so I can arrange for the safe disposal of..." She checked herself, and added, "Pendragon's remains."

"Of course," replied Howard, composing himself. He spent a few minutes signing the paperwork and discussing arrangements with Carol before a visibly shaken Charles joined him to walk back to the preparation area.

After walking in awkward silence for a while, Charles cleared his throat. "I'm so sorry. I know how much Pendragon meant to you."

Howard accepted Charles's condolences with a wry smile. "He lived to compete, and he died to compete. I can think of no better way for him to go." As they walked on a little further, Howard added, "He will be hard to replace."

"That's true, my friend, without a doubt." Charles's eyes twinkled as he added, "But not impossible."

Howard stopped walking and looked at his old friend. "What are you up to, Charlie boy? I know that look, and it usually ends with one of us getting in trouble."

"Let's get back to your prep area, then I'll fill you in on my little scheme." Charles strode off, leaving Howard trailing behind him. Looking over his shoulder, Charles shouted back, "Oh, *do* keep up, Howard!"

Arriving back at the preparation area, Howard hugged Jess, who was fighting back tears. But when he asked her if she was all right to continue, she nodded eagerly. She moved away and started removing Brianna's makeup, ready for the long journey home, their winning performance now hollow and irrelevant.

"I've withdrawn Rhod from the competition, but decided to let him perform his second routine for the audience. I think it would be a fitting tribute to Pendragon and it might cheer everyone up." As she spoke, Geraldine applied heavy clown makeup to Rhoderick's face.

"That's a good idea, love. Everybody enjoys a zombie clown. Even Pendragon used to watch Rhod in the ring, always shaking his head as if he disapproved, but never missing a performance." Howard realised he was smiling at the memories. "See? Working already," he pointed at his own face.

Helping his wife dress Rhoderick in the large blue and yellow quartered overalls and oversized bright red shoes, Howard almost forgot his tragic loss. He was here to compete, to put on a show, to entertain and, like his departed friend, he was a professional. There'd be plenty of time to mourn when they got home.

As Geraldine led Rhoderick away towards the ring, Howard heard the heavy clunk and high-pitched beeping of the electromagnetic cage locks sliding into place. Glancing towards the table, he assumed Jess was returning Brianna to the security of her cage, but both were still seated there. Jess was struggling to pull Brianna's pink jogging bottoms over the dead woman's knees.

Swinging round to face the small containment cage, Howard came face-to-face with his oldest friend standing in it with an expression of serene calm upon his face. "I told you I was hatching a scheme," Charles said, a mischievous smile on his lips. In one hand he held a syringe. An empty bottle, which Howard recognised as anaesthetic normally employed to calm down hyperactive zombies, fell from the other.

"What are you doing, Charles?" Howard questioned his friend while he inspected the locking mechanism. It was securely fastened, deliberately so. Charles had chosen to lock himself in.

"I found this... sleepy juice in that lovely... ZMT's bag when she was busy doing the paper...work." Charles paused several times as his anaesthetised brain struggled to find the right words. "I've already had a little bit... just to numb the... thingies... senses."

"Jess! Get security here. Please tell them to bring a skeleton key." Not taking his eyes off his friend, he continued, "Take Brianna with you, please." Hearing Jess and Brianna scurry away, Howard turned his attention back to Charles.

"They won't get here in time," the man stated, almost for his own benefit. "I've thought about this," Charles airily waves the syringe around, "since Sara died, I'm already dead inside. So why not finish the job?" Waving a dismissive hand at Howard, who was about to argue with him, he continued, "I was going to go... quietly at home, but then that's never been my style...has it?"

Trying again to interrupt his friend and stall his plans, Howard stepped closer to the cage. Charles shushed him, like a drunk returning home late to a quiet house. "I'm trying to make a fuckin' farewell speech here, Howard. Don't interrupt me... where was I... oh yes. Not my style. But today I saw a chance, a chance to have another go, to live... or maybe die... Sara's dream. You losing Pendragon opened a unique opportunity. *Carpe diem*, Howard. *Carpe diem.* Make me Pendragon's replacement." With that,

Charles stuck the needle into the crook of his arm, pushing the plunger down in one smooth movement.

"No!" Grabbing the steel cage door, Howard shook it violently. Charles's vacant eyes stared back at him for a fleeting moment. Then his body went limp, crumpling to the ground.

Screaming for help, Howard continued shaking the steel cage. In the distance he heard people running, their heavy boots smacking heavily on the concrete, but he knew it was too late. With a dose that large, Charles would die in seconds. He leaned against the cage, his fingers interlocking with the mesh, and stared helplessly at the second of his friends to die that day.

Unseen hands pulled him away and he released his grip so the security detail could unlock the cage. Howard stood alone, shocked at what he had just witnessed, distraught at the loss of someone so close. Trying to get his thoughts in order, he watched events unfold around him in slow motion. It was only when security unfurled a large white sheet to cover the corpse that normal service resumed. He realised then that there was work to do, a friend's final wish to be fulfilled.

"Hey! That body's mine!" he shouted at the security detail awaiting another gurney. "It was verbally bequeathed before his death." Looking around, he spotted Geraldine standing open-mouthed in the crowd gathered around him. "Geraldine!"

As his wife made her way towards him, with Rhoderick close behind, Howard ducked into the cage to check the body. As he suspected, it was still warm. But the clock was ticking. As Geraldine appeared behind him, he said, "Get Jess to help you get Brianna and Rhoderick back on the truck, then come back with a transport bag. If we can get Charles's body into the truck's chilled compartment we can extend the time before tissue degradation starts to perhaps five hours. That'll be long enough to allow us to work on him overnight."

Howard couldn't help but smile to himself. Charles was going to get a second chance at winning that elusive small gold statue. And just as it looked like the end for Howard's generation, that no one could compete with the moneymen of the east, a dream team fell into his lap. A popular former owner turned Zombie paired with one of the country's best young trainers. Charles was going to have a new lease of life; all they had to do was seize the day.

Concrete Skull

"How are you Rose? Is the food as bad as everyone says?" Dr Thorne sat at the only table in the spacious interview room, a thick loose-leaf file open in front of her. The edges of her mouth turned upwards in a professional smile her eyes failed to reflect. They were too busy scrutinizing Rose's face, trying to gauge her mood.

"Well it isn't going to win a Michelin star, but it's okay. Not as good as home cooking, but I guess that's not going to matter after tomorrow." Rose swaggered confidently to the vacant chair opposite Dr Thorne, her manacles clinking softly as she moved.

As Rose sat down, Dr Thorne nodded to the burly female guard loitering beside the thick steel door, signalling for her to leave. The guard couldn't disguise her look of relief as she pulled the door shut. She was now free to grab a coffee from a nearby machine before sitting in relative comfort in the next room, from where she could view proceedings through two mirrored observation windows dominating the wall opposite the doctor. There was nothing worse than standing in the corner during a psychiatrist's interview, especially one with a death-row inmate. The doctor was usually only interested in getting some salacious detail to help sell their book while the prisoner would either protest their obvious innocence – there are no guilty prisoners – or boast about the bodies the authorities had never found in an attempt to get a stay of execution.

"Got a smoke, Doc?" Rose smiled at her pretty visitor.

"You know the answer to that, Rose." Dr Thorne sat back in the hard plastic chair, folding her arms loosely across her chest. She didn't want her patient dictating the conversation, so she consciously withdrew herself, closing her body language, but keeping her focus on Rose's face. She saw the small flicker of frustration cross the woman's countenance as facial muscles tightened in anger; then, as quickly as it had appeared, it was gone. Maybe she was finally gaining some control over her demons.

"It's forbidden for visitors to bring contraband into this facility." Rose recited the signs posted around the prison's reception area and the

47

visiting rooms in a mocking tone.

"So why do you ask? You know the rules. Do you think they don't apply to you, is that it?" Sitting forward again, Dr Thorne placed her elbows on the brushed steel table top, interlacing her fingers just below her chin, pressuring the woman opposite for a response.

Rose met her stare for a brief moment, then broke away laughing softly as if she'd enjoyed a private joke. "And here's me, thinking you came for a social visit. Then you start with the psycho-babble bullshit. You're going to ask about my father, about my childhood, and then you'll get onto the subject of sex. What is it with you psychiatrists that make you so obsessed with other people's sex lives? Were you too nerdy at college to see any action? Do you need to hear other people talk about it to get off? Is that it, Doctor?"

She lounged confidently back in her chair, fixing her eyes on the well-dressed doctor. Rose could see the other woman's discomfort, noting that she'd retreated a little. The doctor no longer sat forward, but had assumed a neutral, upright position while shuffling some of the papers in the folder. Rose noticed the doctor's face had flushed a deeper shade of red and decided to press home her advantage. "Do you want to hear what goes on in here? Fifty shades of prison grey. Even that ugly bitch guard outside has her fair share of admirers." She gave a seductive smile towards the darkened windows and pulled a provocative pose before laughing aloud.

"And what about you, Rose? Have you got admirers?" Dr Thorne cut in quickly, eager to turn the conversation back to her patient. "Exactly how popular is a woman who cuts off her husband's head before slaughtering her own children?"

Rose remained silent for a few moments, contemplating the question. Dr Thorne noticed the faraway look in her pale blue eyes as she stared down at the table and wondered if Rose was thinking of that horrific night. Remembering those poor children, dead in their beds, their corpses mutilated beyond recognition. A smile crept across Rose's features as she looked up and met the doctor's gaze, "I do okay. Fame has its privileges, even in here."

"Fame? Is that what you call it?" asked Dr Thorne sarcastically, she searched through the file looking for the crime scene photographs. "I don't think 'fame' is the right word. You're hardly a celebrity. Even in *this* facility there are more renowned killers than you." Locating the photograph she wanted, Dr Thorne placed it face down in front of Rose, she couldn't bring herself to look at it. Besides, the image had been burned into her brain; she couldn't close her eyes without seeing the bloody sheets and rag doll bodies of the two boys. "If you have anything, it's notoriety. You don't even get pity in the outside world. Even the most charitable do-gooders despise you." She fixed Rose with an analytical stare, searching for any clue that would tell her what the convicted killer was thinking.

Rose shrugged and began biting her thumbnail, causing Dr Thorne to smile inwardly. Rose bit her thumbnails when she was out of her comfort zone; it was a trait Dr Thorne had noticed during the many hearings and court appearances she'd attended while following the case. She'd done a similar thing when she was a child, until her father had painted her nails with petrol and threatened to set light to them if she continued. It was her earliest memory of her father and one that had set the tone for most of her childhood memories. The years of bullying had, by the time Thorne was old enough to understand, taken their toll on her mother, who'd been a broken woman. When her husband turned his anger on her daughter she had just looked on with empty eyes, no doubt just glad it wasn't her body taking the beating, her mind being torn apart by his barbed insults.

It was why, when Thorne left for college, she never went back.

"Sometimes, in the really dark moments, I despise myself," Rose mumbled, her voice barely audible across the table. "But then sometimes I wish I'd kept killing; slaughtering the weak. Destroying their innocence before they too became corrupt and oppressive; bent to his will." Rose's voice had risen to a crescendo as she leant forward and spat the words into Dr Thorne's face. "I'm sure you understand me, with your college education and your perfect life. Riding the endless merry-go-round of fund-raisers and awards dinners, and we mustn't forget those oh so important weekends away, while all the time hiding from your past."

Dr Thorne ignored the reference to her past. Rose was fishing. Testing her resolve. Looking for a way of attacking her; a way of getting under her skin. But, she wasn't about to let that happen. Instead she focused on Rose's first statement.

"Why do you despise yourself, Rose?" Hearing the tension in her own voice, she forced herself to take a couple of deep breaths. She'd known all along this final meeting was going to be tense, maybe even dangerous, but she had to come. She needed answers. In her own way, she needed to find some closure. She'd visited the crime scene, had witnessed first-hand the barbaric nature of the murders, attended countless hearings and appeals, interviewed Rose at length and tomorrow, a little over eight years after that horrendous November night, she would attend her execution. But today was about closure or possibly, at least for Rose, redemption.

Rose had calmed again, a long drawn out sigh escaped her lips. Her eyes were seemingly looking inward, as though searching for an answer written on a wall somewhere in the dark catacombs of her mind. "I despise myself for getting caught before I completed my task. I despise myself for failing God; it was he who told me to rid the world of man's evil. And men are evil. My father, the upstanding pillar of the community who dished out justice during the week, attended church on Sunday while all the time he beat his own child in the name of God. His high-and-mighty friends coming around to watch him horsewhip me, telling themselves they were combatting Lucifer's evil machinations. But really, they just got off on it." Again, Rose had built herself into a frenzy as she spoke. But now she fell silent, her head bowed, her unkempt hair falling forward, obscuring her face. "I despise myself for not killing every one of his sick disciples."

"So why did you kill your husband and the two boys? What did they do so wrong that you had to slaughter them while they slept?" Dr Thorne knew the answer; she'd asked the same question a hundred times over the years, it had become part of the process, almost a ritual, in getting Rose to talk.

Rose looked up at Dr Thorne and smiled. Not the deranged smile of a psychotic killer, but the warm smile of a friend sharing a chat over a cup of coffee. "I love your nails. Such a rich colour."

Dr Thorne returned the smile and replied, "Thank you. It's Poppy Red. I had them done at a place in the same block as my office."

"There's nothing that fancy near my office, just a broom cupboard and an execution suite." Rose genuinely laughed at her own gallows humour as if it took her by surprise. "You always look so pretty, Dr Thorne, with your colourful nails and stylish hair. I bet you can take your pick when it comes to men — doctors, lawyers or maybe just a bit of dirty fun with a gardener? You don't look like you ever had much time for relationships, too busy building a career and a reputation. And, of course, writing a book about me." Rose paused for a second or two then asked, "So tell me doctor, do I die at the end?"

Dr Thorne felt a little self-conscious under Rose's line of questioning, so she shuffled the pages in her file. The photograph she'd placed in front of Rose remained face down on the table, and she left it there. "I think it's important to keep myself looking neat and presentable. I guess it's a pride thing." Dr Thorne again chose not to answer the more intimate parts of Rose's questions.

"Or maybe it's a way of hiding the real Dr Thorne, the mask of perfection hiding a troubled soul. The beautiful, successful woman on the outside while inside the ugly little girl still hides away, lost in her own world. A world few ever understood." Rose picked up the photograph, her manacles clattering loudly on the desk's metallic surface as she held it up. "I've seen this one before, but it's always good to relive old times. You know that the whole thing was all over in less than ten minutes?" Rose placed the photograph face up on the table and looked directly into the doctor's eyes, "But of course you do. Your next question will focus on the bloody marks on the walls... you're all so fucking predictable!"

"Okay, Rose, I'll bite. Why did you make those marks on the wall?"

A smile spread slowly across Rose's face. When she eventually spoke her words were slow and deliberate. "I'd run out of marker pen."

Dr Thorne remained impassive and simply stared defiantly across the table at the killer. "Change the record, Rosie," she said deliberately using the nickname Rose's father had for her. The response was immediate.

"How fucking *dare* you use that name! I hate it. I hate you, you fucking stuck up bitch. What gives you the right to come in here and mess with my head? You want to know something? I'm looking forward to tomorrow because I'll never have to see your smug face again."

As she shouted at Thorne, Rose climbed to her feet. Dr Thorne noted with satisfaction that Rose had completely lost control of her emotions. White spittle appeared around the inmate's mouth as she screamed more obscenities at the psychologist. Thorne felt droplets hit her face, but she held her ground maintaining, her defiant stare until the woman opposite started to calm down.

Then she calmly repeated her question.

"Why did you make those marks in blood on the wall? On the wall of the bedroom your sons shared?"

"It was a message to the Devil." Rose was agitated. Dr Thorne had got her blood boiling and she was no longer in the mood to play games or indulge in friendly chit-chat.

"The police tried to identify the language, but drew a blank. It's not an ancient language, at least nothing discovered, and the symbols meant nothing to either the Smithsonian or British Library." Dr Thorne paused for a moment to allow the information to sink in, then asked, "Can you explain that?"

"It was a message from God to the fallen angel, Lucifer. I do not presume to understand the language of the angels. I'm just a humble mouthpiece. I simply drew what God told me to draw," stated Rose as if it were an undeniable fact. The blood-stained symbols were almost unintelligible, bearing no resemblance to anything close to a known language. They appeared, instead, to be the mad rantings of a sociopath who, unable to navigate the real world, had created their own fantasy one.

"So God just placed these images in your head for you to draw at the murder scene…"

"It was never a murder scene," Rose interrupted. "It was a battlefield."

"And you just copied them from memory, is that it?" Dr Thorne ignored the interruption. "So if this is God's work, why would he demand you cut the victims' faces off? The God I was taught to believe in would not demand such violence against children."

Rose jumped to her feet, knocking the flimsy plastic chair over in her haste. She lurched against the table, then regained her balance and shuffled away, the shackles adding a surreal, comic jingling sound to her movements. "I thought you smarter than this, Dr Thorne. Maybe I've wasted my precious time talking to you when you've obviously struggled to understand the simplest things. As I have told you many times before, I cut their devious little faces off to unmask the demons that lurked behind them."

"Surely the demon could be unmasked in a less literal sense. I don't believe God told you to slice the skin away from their skulls. I think you twisted his words to suit your own insane desires. In fact, Rose, I think the God you hear is just the inane ramblings of a truly twisted and deeply psychotic mind." Dr Thorne deliberately tried to antagonise Rose, she needed to discover the evil concealed inside and, like a wounded animal hiding in its deep, dark lair, it needed to be lured out.

Rose now stood before one of the mirrored observation windows, her back to Dr Thorne. There was a long moment of awkward silence during which Thorne felt too uncomfortable even to flick though the open file. Rose was, to say the least, unpredictable. Had she driven her too far, too quickly? That could be dangerous. Dr Thorne found herself holding her breath. She exhaled, the sound loud inside her own head.

Then Rose began to laugh. It was deep and slow, unlike her normal cheery laughter, which danced lightly off her tongue. "Is that your professional diagnosis, Doctor? 'Truly twisted and deeply psychotic," Rose paused, her head tilted back as if considering the words carefully, then added, "I kinda like it."

Dr Thorne stood up and stepped out from behind the table. She wiped her sweaty palms against her expensively-clad hips and casually walked across the room to stand next to Rose. Being careful not to get too close, she studied the woman's profile. Rose remained still, as she stared into the darkened window, admiring her own reflected image.

"So what do you see when you look at your reflection? Do you see the loving mother and dutiful wife, or the sadistic monster? Which is it, Rose?"

"The loving mother," Rose's voice was little more than a whisper. "They were my children and I loved them, but they were also instruments of evil. I couldn't just stand by and watch as it consumed them from within; burning away their souls until they became mere vessels from which Lucifer's minions could wreak their havoc. Their death, like my husband's, was an act of mercy."

Rose turned her head towards Dr Thorne and, after a moment of contemplation, added, "What do you see in your reflection, Doctor Thorne? A crime fighting superheroine who matched her wits against the machinations of a psychotic mind while maintaining a sexual aloofness that attracted men and women in equal numbers?" Rose smiled, but Thorne felt no warmth in it. "Or do you see the real you, the one you've spent your entire adult life running from?"

Dr Thorne turned away, but couldn't help but glance at her reflection in the shiny black glass. For a second she had looked like a superheroine in her charcoal gray Yves Saint Laurent suit with her recently styled blonde hair falling in loose waves across her shoulders and her weapon-like immaculately manicured nails. It was all designed to draw attention while serving as a warning that she was not to be messed with. Yet this tough, confident exterior was built on a fragile framework of wreckage, the sleek professional image built to hide the ugly scars of her youth. College, her career, the endless moving between cities: all had been designed to get her physically and emotionally away from her childhood.

The image Dr Thorne saw when she stared through the superficial reflection was of a little girl hiding behind the door every time her father came home drunk. A girl so scared to go home that she often hung around the school library either to study or just read, often heading for the shelves housing the criminology books. She hadn't known it then, but those were her first few tentative steps in her escape plan. From there she'd discovered criminal psychology and by the time she'd turned thirteen she'd mapped out her future career path. Shortly after her eighteenth birthday she'd packed her bags and left home in the middle of the night in search of a job with which to fund her education.

"Well, Doctor Thorne?" Rose ran her fingers through her hair and pouted at her reflection. She pulled a series of faces as if she were posing for a high-class fashion magazine, but then stopped, as if unhappy with what she saw.

"The issue is not what I see. This is about you, not me." Dr Thorne forced her gaze away from her reflection, focusing on Rose.

"On the contrary, Dr Thorne, this is very much about you." Rose turned to face her visitor, "We are very similar, you and me. We both came from abusive homes, we both ran away at eighteen in search of our dreams, in search of a better life and, dare I say, our own brand of revenge. I became an avenging angel doing God's work on earth, while you searched the minds of insane killers hoping to find answers to your own questions."

Dr Thorne looked into Rose's face and contemplated whether it was worth challenging her on the whole 'God' issue again, but decided against it. Instead she looked back at the mirrored panel in front of her and ran her fingers through her hair before pulling a sultry pout.

Rose giggled briefly, then her face became serious again and she said, "You were always better at that than me and it made me so jealous of you. You always were the pretty one, the intelligent one, the one people noticed and I hated you for it. I hated you and your perfect life. There, are you happy now?"

The two women looked at their near identical reflections. Rose's countenance, bereft of makeup, looked tired, her hair hanging limp and greasy, while Thorne looked tanned and healthy, her deftly applied makeup accentuating her beauty. After a while, Dr Thorne whispered, "Well I suppose you're happy that you've ruined that. Tomorrow they execute you, so what becomes of me?"

"Yeah, I guess I am. Being happy is not a feeling I'm used to, so I'm not sure. But I know I hate your success and ruining that for you will please me." Rose shuffled back to the table and deliberately sat in the chair Dr Thorne had vacated. She flicked idly through the file, a distant smile on her face as if she was looking through a family album and remembering days out and long dead relatives. Without looking up she said, "I know I deserve to die for what I did, but I also know the part you played in my crimes... do you?" Rose looked at Thorne, her eyebrow arched questioningly.

"I had no part in your vile crimes. It was your DNA and fingerprints at the scene, their blood on your clothes, not mine." Dr Thorne smiled confidently back at Rose.

"Yes, it is. I can't deny that. But it's not exclusively my DNA and fingerprints — I share those with you, Dr Rose Thorne!"

The confident smile fell from Dr Thorne's face like a theatrical mask falling away to reveal the actor beneath. "I h… have no idea what you're talking about." Flustered, Dr Thorne hurried to gather the scattered reports and photographs.

Rose held up a photograph and said, "So that's not you then?" The picture was a police mug shot, an attractive blonde standing in front of a height board holding a card with a row of numbers on it.

Dr Thorne stared at the picture, the scattered files forgotten. It was her, but how?

"Not one of our best shots, granted, but we had just murdered our family. That's got to take it out of a girl! I've known all along I wasn't doing God's work. Why would he need me to fight demons? I may be nuts, but I ain't fucking crazy... I knew it was your voice."

Dr Thorne still stared at the photograph in disbelief. The forgotten files gradually vanished, evaporating into the ether. Eventually that photograph vanished too, leaving Dr Thorne to stare into the eyes of her doppelgänger as she finally realised the truth.

Rose continued, "Always in the background, goading me on, living a fantasy life, my fantasy life. While I just took all the shit; the guilt of my childhood, the blame for the killings, the public hatred of a child killer. But you could never walk away, never escape my head," she raised her hands and vaguely indicated the four plain concrete walls, her manacles now gone. "But it's all over now. Tomorrow they will execute the... how did you describe me? Oh yes, the notorious child killer, Rose Thorne." She gave a hollow, mirthless laugh, "So you see, I have no more need of a fantasy life and therefore I have no more need of you." Rose closed her eyes and leant back in the chair, signalling the visit was over.

Dr Thorne remained standing next to the empty table until it too faded away, then turned and walked to the door, her knock echoing around the empty room as she took a last look at Rose. The door opened quietly and she stepped through.

After a few minutes, lights came on behind the two mirrored windows and illuminated the small interview room. The image of a middle-aged man wearing a white doctor's coat appeared simultaneously in each window. Rose smiled and greeted the man with a cheery wave, "Hello, Doctor Jackson."

"Hello, Doctor Thorne," replied the man with a polite professional nod.

"I'm afraid you missed her, Doctor Jackson. She's gone. There's only me left."

"Where did she go, Rose?"

"She's going home to take a bath, put on one of her expensive dresses, and then hang herself from a wooden beam in her upmarket townhouse," Rose chuckled softly, then added, "I imagine."

Eating For Two

Rosie lay face down in darkness. The side of her face pressed numbly against a rough stone floor and her right arm, stretching upwards, had a heavy iron manacle fastened around the wrist. The chain was securely bolted to the wall, only allowing her to move a few yards in each direction.

Her shoulder felt stiff and lifeless. Rosie attempted to move it a little so she could sit upright, but her muscles had seized around the joint, locking it tight. She used her left arm to push herself into a sitting position; the movement caused her right shoulder to crack as her weight redistributed on the end of the chain.

Rosie stifled a cry as sharp pain shot through her shoulder. Instinctively, her left hand came up to clutch it, trying to stem the keen, searing pain. Without her left arm to support it, Rosie's weakened body toppled over, causing her weight to pull mercilessly on the unforgiving chain.

This time Rosie was powerless to stifle the scream that erupted from deep within her: the pain ripped through her shoulder as her upper body swung helplessly. She desperately kicked her bare feet across the straw that provided a sparse covering to the tiny cell floor. Finally, she managed to get enough purchase to push herself backwards until she was up against the wall. The chain's solid links clinked and creaked as it fell slack, and Rosie gently pulled her arm into her side. Tears welled up in her eyes, stinging them: a solitary tear rolled gently down her cheek. She felt it as it ran down the side of her nose before reaching her lip, its saltiness stinging an open wound. She used the back of her hand to wipe it away.

Rosie hadn't cried for days, maybe a week. She'd lost track of time, lying alone in the dark. How long was it since she'd been so violently dragged from the safety of Gary's arms?

Thoughts of Gary caused her to utter another guttural snivel. She placed her hands on her swollen belly. As if sensing its mother's distress the baby gave a soft kick. Rosie gently rubbed the bump, making soothing sounds through the tears.

Gary had insisted on taking her for a relaxing cruise before their son's birth. He'd hired a yacht for the week so they could explore the small islands and waterways that constituted this part of the estuary. For three days it had been idyllic, just the two of them, with no distractions. They had spent the warm lazy days sunbathing, swimming and eating freshly prepared meals on the deck. Gary spent the evenings lying with his ear pressed against her belly, waiting for his boy to kick, while they planned their future together.

One night, it all changed. They'd spotted an old jetty which had probably once belonged to one of the small farms that worked the fertile fields surrounding the river. Now most of those farms had gone, leaving deserted buildings scattered across the landscape. Having tied the yacht to the most secure-looking part of the dilapidated woodwork, she and Gary had enjoyed a light meal while bathing in the warm orange glow of the sunset, before retiring to bed.

Rosie had found sleep difficult; unable to get comfortable in the small bunk, she had listened to the gentle sounds of water lapping against the yacht's hull. Then she heard what sounded like a footstep on the deck above. It was quickly followed by another.

She shook Gary's shoulder, desperately trying to wake him without attracting the attention of whoever was treading across the foredeck. Just as he began to stir, a dark figure appeared in the open hatchway. Another followed as their unwanted visitor dropped down into the tiny cabin.

Rough hands had grabbed her wrists, dragging her from the bunk onto the floor. In the half-light of the cabin she'd watched helplessly as two figures jumped on Gary. There'd been a brief struggle, then one of the assailants had raised their arm high above their head. The metal pipe fleetingly reflected the crowded cabin's available light before crashing down into the melee. There was a sickeningly dull crack and all movement stopped.

Rosie had screamed in a futile bid to summon help. Her senses struggled to respond to the terrifying reality that her unborn baby's father had been brutally bludgeoned before her eyes. Just as she began sucking in air for another hopeless scream, a fist hurtled out of the darkness. Its impact on the point of Rosie's delicate jaw had snapped her head backwards, followed by darkness pouring into her head as she lost consciousness.

She had woken up chained to the wall, still wearing her silk maternity pyjamas, with no idea how long she'd been out for. That had been a long time ago now, but when you're cold, hungry and in pain, chained to a wall in a tiny cell with no windows, a single minute can feel like a lifetime.

Occasionally, her captors had come to check on her. They were always dressed in crudely cut hoods, similar to those worn by medieval executioners made from rough hessian sacking. Only the lower halves of their faces were visible. The bare-chested men (Rosie thought there were three of them), all had strange symbols tattooed above their left breast. The marks were amateurish, as though self-drawn during a drunken party or some bizarre initiation ceremony. On their last visit they had left her with a bottle of water and some soup with the consistency of badly-made porridge.

The fourth person had been a scrawny woman wearing an ill-fitting T-shirt and the same head covering. She had roughly examined Rosie's swollen belly, then, appearing satisfied the baby was still alive, started to leave. Rosie had tried to appeal to the woman's maternal instincts, pleading with her to let her go so she could get medical help. But the woman's only response was to slap Rosie's face before leaving through the heavy wooden door without as much as a second glance in Rosie's direction.

Now Rosie sat with her back against the rough stone wall, crying uncontrollably. She was hungry, frustrated and hurting. She was wailing for her dead husband, but above all she was crying for her unborn child. As his mother she was responsible for his well-being, but even before he'd been born, she'd failed him. She was the one who should be supplying him with everything he needed to grow, to develop, to thrive. But here she was, starving to death goodness knows where, held captive by a bunch of sick freaks.

Why had she agreed to Gary's little trip? What right did she have to go sailing so far away from civilisation when she was so close to giving birth? What the fuck had she been thinking?

If these monsters killed her, then, she reasoned, she probably had it coming. Gary junior, though, certainly didn't deserve to die with her. Rosie stopped crying, suddenly aware that for the first time she had given her son a name. She rubbed her belly. "Hello, Gary junior," she said in a hushed, rasping whisper. Her dry, cracked lips were barely able to form the words. Rosie couldn't help but smile as she looked down at her swollen belly through sore, red-rimmed eyes.

The sound of footsteps outside made Rosie look up, the smile never leaving her face as the door swung open. The two men who entered the room wore masks as usual. The first man's sacking had ridden up on top of his head with the seam forming two vertical points. "Ah... you must be

Batman come to rescue me," Rosie whispered.

The second man stepped into view. Rosie smiled up at them both defiantly, "And you brought Robin with you." Her smile vanished as her attempt to laugh brought on a choking cough that wrung her lungs out and twisted her empty stomach into a series of dry retching cramps. She fell onto her side, drawing her legs up to her bump. Her right arm remained in the air, the iron manacle chafing the flesh away from her bony wrist.

Batman grabbed a handful of Rosie's once luscious auburn hair and pulled her head up so her face was no more than a couple of inches from his. She looked into the rough eyeholes cut into the sack, seeing dark piggy eyes staring back at her. The dilated pupils filled them with a blank glassy blackness as they flicked frantically back and forth. His mouth twisted into a leering smile as Rosie cried out in pain, his rancid foul-smelling breath causing her to recoil despite his strong grip on her hair.

The other man unlocked the chain at the wall. He yanked hard on it, pulling Rosie's arm backwards. Renewed pain exploded through her shoulder. The force tore her from the other man's grip, leaving him clutching a fistful of long hair. The men laughed hysterically while Rosie rolled about on the floor in an attempt to relieve the pressure on her damaged shoulder. The man dragged her by the chain through the doorway and across an uneven concrete floor, every inch of which ripped away her expensive pyjamas, tearing the top layer of skin from her buttocks and back as she instinctively tried to shield her unborn child from the unforgiving surface.

"Hey! Stop that! The woman and her child must live." The voice, rough and uneducated, belonged to a woman, but Rosie was too battered and disorientated to see where it had come from. She was just thankful that her burning slide into hell had stopped. She lay on her side, curled up in the foetal position.

In the distance, somewhere outside the locked doors of her conscious mind, Rosie could hear voices. She couldn't make out the words, nor did she care. She felt sure her shoulder must have been dislocated. Her delicate powder blue pyjamas were hanging from her in blood-stained tatters, and her back was ablaze with a thousand jagged cuts.

Rough hands hauled her upright and she was half walked, half dragged towards the hooded female figure standing by a set of large double doors. As her captors dragged her closer, Rosie realised that it was the woman who'd slapped her face the day before — or was it longer ago than that?

Rosie's escort stopped before the figure and stood with her standing unsteadily between them. The woman walked behind her and she felt a hand brush across the raw wounds on her shoulder.

Rosie flinched involuntarily and immediately cursed herself for the display of vulnerability. As the woman came back into view, Rosie fixed her with what she hoped was a cold defiant stare. The two empty black voids in the hood just returned her gaze, almost daring her to continue. The silent inhumanity of the featureless hood taunted her.

Rosie couldn't sustain her defiance and, after a few moments, she closed her eyes and let her head drop forward as they removed the ruined pyjamas from her battered body. She felt the sting as the material pulled free of her torn, bloody flesh.

Rosie was too tired to resist. She was cold and naked, and weak from hunger. All she could feel was excruciating pain. Her mind was still struggling to comprehend the shock and grief of seeing Gary, her soul mate, brutally murdered back on their rented yacht. The only thing stopping her from lying down, closing her eyes and never waking up was her unborn son. Gary's son.

The woman produced a rolled-up piece of material which she unravelled to reveal a large dress. It was probably once brilliant white, but now it was grubby grey, with several large, foul-looking stains. The woman slid it up Rosie's arms and pulled it over her head. Then she tugged it down over the large prenatal bump, until the hem was just above Rosie's knees. Rosie could feel the cotton adhere to the dampness of the exposed cuts on her back, made more noticeable by the dress stretching to accommodate her swollen belly.

The hooded woman took a step back and looked Rosie over as if she were trying her out for a new dress in some fancy boutique. She tried to fasten a couple of the buttons that ran up the bodice, but Rosie's swollen breasts refused to be confined within the tight material. The woman shrugged, accepting defeat, then opened the large double doors and stepped swiftly into the darkness of the night. A firm push in the small of her back signalled that Rosie should follow her.

Rosie stumbled through the open doorway. The flimsy dress she now wore offered little protection against the night's chill. She felt the late evening breeze gently pushing the dress against her damp back, making her feel even colder. Tiny goose bumps formed on her arms as she followed the skinny woman, accompanied by the two hooded men walking on either side of her. 'Batman' held the chain, tugging it hard if her pace slackened. Neither man spoke.

The group walked briskly for a few minutes, the pale moonlight casting an eerie glow over the landscape as they followed a well-worn farm track away from the barn in which she'd been imprisoned. Rosie became aware of people talking in the distance, and, for a few moments, thoughts of help, of rescue, filled her foggy mind. She made ready to shout, to scream and holler as if her life depended on it, but with a crushing realisation, Rosie noticed more hooded figures standing in the shadows at the edge of the track.

The woman led her past the assembled crowd and they fell into line behind her. Through the trees up ahead, Rosie saw a bright orange fire illuminating the sky, sparks dancing above the flames as the rising air bore them skyward. She tasted acrid wood smoke sticking in her dry throat, which felt like the smoke's tendrils were reaching out to choke her. She began to cough, but firm hands pushed her onwards.

More hooded figures joined the procession as it neared the large clearing in which the fire burned. Rosie guessed there must be about thirty of them now gathered around the crackling blaze. The reality was that she just didn't care. She was in no condition to escape a single one of them.

Rosie peered around the clearing, trying to get her bearings. In the firelight she saw that the hooded figures dancing around her were a mix of men, women, and bizarrely, even children. Some appeared elderly; one walked with a pronounced limp and leant heavily on a carved wooden stick. The men all had bare chests, while the women wore T-shirts; one had on a white bikini top that Rosie recognised as being hers. She'd bought it in a little boutique especially for this holiday.

Close to the fire there were two wooden fenceposts driven into the ground about four feet apart. Batman dragged Rosie towards these sturdy looking posts. Her mind could only imagine the horrors awaiting her. She tried to resist, but the weight of the chain pulled at her injured shoulder and the manacle tore into her flesh. He tugged on the chain with one vicious flick and she stumbled forward, crying out as her knees slammed into the dirt. Unseen hands seized her, pulling her upright before securing her hands to chains attached to each post.

"Get off me!" Rosie kicked out in desperation, but her best efforts just bounced harmlessly off her assailants' shins. Her frustration boiled over into a frantic and frenzied assault on the woman securing her damaged arm above her head. "I said, get the fuck off me." She bit the only part off the woman that she could reach, her teeth tearing through the thin cotton and into the soft fatty tissue below. The woman recoiled with a scream, clutching her breast. Rosie spat the bloodied ball of cotton from her mouth. As it hit the ground, the woman's nipple rolled free of its folds.

"She's a feisty one," a tall figure of a man stepped in front of her. "Look at the defiance in 'er face. We'd do well to keep this un." Then he slapped her hard across the cheek and once more Rosie slumped into unconsciousness.

Rosie awoke some time later, finding herself secured to both posts by chains attached to her wrists. Through the thin cotton of the dress she felt the contrast between the fire's intense heat on her front and the cold night air on her back. Huge logs were burning well on the fire, the thick dark smoke drifting into her face. It obscured her vision, stinging her already sore eyes and causing them to fill with viscous tears that stuck to her eyelashes. Through the haze Rosie could just about make out the silhouette of a large pig roasting over the flickering flames.

The pig had been impaled on a long steel rod which reflected the dancing flames. This skewer rested on two purpose built Y-shaped wooden supports. Rosie watched as two young men slowly turned it, gently revolving the massive chunk of meat. The other hooded figures stood in a loose circle around the fire. The young woman whom Rosie had bitten stood on the other side of the fire, clutching a wad of material to her now exposed breast. She stared back at Rosie, a look of hatred on her face.

The emptiness of Rosie's belly had begun to tie her insides in knots. The first faint smells of the meat slowly cooking over the fire were beginning to reach her nostrils, borne on the gentle breeze. The fire cast a circle of warm secure light amongst the night's dark shadows, lighting up the skewered meat as if it were a prized exhibit in a museum. Rosie stood transfixed, the crackling fire seducing her senses with the aroma of real cooked meat... meat she could almost taste. Meat she could consume, devour, digest and then pass to the new life growing inside her.

Rosie watched as the meat was slowly turned. The pig's face turned towards her, but there was no long snout protruding from the large muscular head, as she had expected. Instead, Rosie found herself gazing into the face of a man. Rosie looked on with disbelief, so confused by the image before her that at first she couldn't react. Convinced that hunger and captivity were conspiring to deceive her, she tried screwing up her face so she could peer through the heat and smoke at the roasting pig as it continued to rotate. The spindle completed a full revolution, the face coming back into view. This time there was no conspiracy, no trick caused by the deceptive dance of light and shadow.

Rosie's hysterical screams filled the night air as she stared into the burnt and blackened face of another human being. The horribly twisted facial features had contorted as the fatty flesh had melted away from the bone beneath. A gruesome toothy grimace played across the eyeless features and yet Rosie, in a state of shock and bewilderment, felt compelled to watch. She could hear her own despairing shrieks in the distance as if were someone else. She stood, tethered in the dark wilderness of human depravity, watching another poor soul being roasted over an open fire and yet she couldn't tear her eyes away.

The man's features were unrecognisable. The thick gelatinous liquid that once formed his eyes had melted away and the previously pale skin was charred and blackened, the hair having been burned away from the smashed and misshapen skull. Yet deep down Rosie knew it was Gary's body on the homemade rotisserie — he'd died of repeated blows to the head, plus the general body size matched.

Rosie wanted, desired, to feel revulsion at the sight of his twisted face and burning flesh. She knew she should look away, vomit, maybe pass out. However she did none of these. Her initial howls of shock and fear had subsided and she now stood quietly staring into the centre of the fire. Part of her, deep within the darkened recesses of her mind, reasoned she was traumatised and undoubtedly going insane, and, therefore not accountable for her actions.

Rosie watched the meat gradually cooking. She heard the hissing, popping sounds as the body's fluids and fat leaked out and dripped into the fire. Occasionally, the flames would flare up as it consumed a particularly large piece of oleaginous matter. The smell of burning flesh, mingling with the pungent smell of wood-smoke, produced a deceptive aroma reminding Rosie of family barbeques in their backyard.

Rosie tried to remember that the succulent looking hog roast was once a living, breathing person. Not just any person, but her loving, caring Gary, the father of her unborn child. Despite that, the stark reality was that Rosie was starving. The more she could smell of that sweet aroma, the louder her stomach rumbled in expectation. Rosie involuntarily ran her tongue across her lips, unaware that she was salivating.

After a while a hooded figure approached the crackling flames. He raised his arm to shield his face from the heat and with one hand rammed a long skewer into Gary's charred and blackened back before retreating. He repeated the action several times before being satisfied and signalled for the removal of the long metal spike from the brackets. The two men who'd been turning the spit now lifted Gary's body, still impaled on the metal rod, over to a picnic-style table.

Other hooded figures followed the two meat bearers as they made their way over to the table. They laid the roasted human carcass carefully across the top as the hooded figures assembled in a half circle around it. The gap in the grouping allowed Rosie a clear view of her lover, now looking like a giant joint of barbecued pork. All stood in silence, their grotesquely deformed half sack faces turning to face Rosie as if awaiting her approval.

She suddenly realised that in this macabre midnight feast, she was the guest of honour. That was why they had forced her into this badly fitting white dress, even if it did gape open to reveal her swollen breasts. So she would be smart for her big date. These psychopaths had chosen to keep her alive and yet had turned Gary into prime, smoked, pulled pork. What Rosie couldn't work out was why?

Then her tiny, unborn child kicked her. Rosie looked down at her distended belly, then back up at the silent gathering crowded around the picnic table. They'd wanted her because she was pregnant.

Maybe this insular community of freaks were so inbred they couldn't have children of their own. They lived out here beyond the physical and moral boundaries of normal society, never moving outside their own gene pool.

The head chef broke the spell holding the crowd in silence by emitting a roaring grunt. He stood behind the wooden picnic table, arms aloft, a knife in one hand and a large two-pronged fork in the other. Once he had their attention he began to carve a strip of flesh from Gary's back. The sharp knife easily cut through the tender meat just above the left buttock. Rosie tried to avert her eyes, but still felt that strange voyeuristic compulsion to watch.

The chef held the six inch strip of meat aloft so the assembled crowd could see it. Then he walked towards Rosie. She followed his approach, powerless to escape and long since having stopped tugging at the chains; it had only served to cause further pain to her injured arm. Finally, the hooded chef stood before her. She couldn't see any detail in his face. The fire, now directly behind him, limned the man as a menacing silhouette. He raised the succulent, warm meat to her lips. Rosie smelled its gentle sweetness and her mouth watered at the thought of its tenderness, her stomach growled, expecting sustenance. Deep inside her traumatised head, her sense of morality wrestled with her survival instincts.

Rosie's host for the evening wiped the strip of meat across her pursed lips before pushing it gently into her mouth. His greasy fingers probed and prised at her clenched teeth, working their way around her gums. She wanted to keep her mouth shut and put a stop to this barbarous charade, but her survival instinct held sway, her sense of morality retreating deeper into her battered psyche.

As she opened her mouth to admit the small morsel, Rosie told herself she was eating for two. She desperately tried to convince herself that this was the last despairing act of a mother who was protecting her child.

The greasy fingers of the monstrous chef fell away, sliding across her chin. Rosie felt the strip of meat on her dry bulbous tongue, but made

64

no effort to chew it. She couldn't tell if this was out of some moral sensibility or just that she found it physically awkward to move her facial muscles.

She felt the warm slippery grease oozing from the small sliver of Gary's flesh lodged inside her mouth. It ran from the corner of her lips and down her neck as she stared straight ahead with unseeing eyes at the crackling fire in front of her.

Then, with slow deliberate movements, Rosie began to chew. She tasted the tanginess of the wood smoke. She found the meat chewy, but not tough, the smokiness forming a pleasant contrast with the meat's mild sweetness. Rosie's chewing became more frenzied as she tried to swallow this new delicacy. The pain that had racked her jaw and arm now forgotten as she greedily devoured the crazy chef's house speciality.

She swallowed the first piece of human flesh and stared with wide, wild eyes at the dark figure standing before her. "More!" She forced the word out, barely recognising her own voice; it was low and gravelly. It pulled at her throat like a barb had caught in her gullet.

A soft laugh came from the silhouetted figure and he stepped forward to offer her another piece of the spit-roasted human hog. "I'm glad you see it our way. We've got plans for you and your unborn." Rosie was assailed by his foul breath even over the stench of his sweat. The assembled mob of faceless savages was now tearing chunks of flesh from the cooling body. They cheered at his words.

Rosie had tasted forbidden flesh and now craved it. Her unborn child craved it, too. She was torn between the desire to eat and her guilt for surviving. She should be grieving for her partner's murder, his barbaric slaughter. Her mind, struggling to comprehend the harrowing cruelty she had witnessed, ceased to function normally. The caring compassionate part of Rosie, the part that loved unreservedly, and made morally correct decisions, was gone. In its place was a wounded animal, trapped and fighting for its life.

She leant forward, her neck straining to reach the sweet juicy meat on offer. It swung from her captor's fingers, tantalisingly just out of reach. "One more bit. Then you can go back to the cell 'til you give birth. Then we'll decide what to do with you."

The meat swung closer and Rosie opened her cracked and bruised lips. The chef's fingers allowed the meat to fall into her waiting mouth. This time she chewed the meat like a dog given a raw steak. Her most basic primal instinct had taken over. Rosie was now no more than a wild animal and deep down she knew it. Her defiant streak lay shredded by a combination of her hunger and their senseless brutality. A senseless brutality they'd used to kill Gary. A death they had forced her to witness. Rosie was no more a human than these savages. She was theirs to mould, to train, and to keep on a chain just like a yard dog.

The chef took a step towards her and leant in close so he could whisper. "I have a special dish planned for the new arrival. I need something more sophisticated for such a rare, tender treat." He stepped back as Rosie doubled over in pain, an agonising cramp passing through her abdomen and into her thighs.

Rosie felt the fluid run down her thighs, soaking the grubby dress. Momentarily confused, she looked down at the small puddle forming in the mud around her feet. A second spasm shook her body. Rosie doubled over again, desperate to ease the pain. Her arms pulled at the restraints as her legs crumpled.

Her feet danced a frantic jig in the slippery mire as she tried to support her weight. The pain in her grotesquely bent shoulder was unbearable. The muscles around her womb contracted again and Rosie slumped forward, hanging on the chains holding her wrists.

She raised her head, attempting to focus on the hooded figure standing before her. His laughing image spun before her eyes, and in that moment of surreal peace before she fainted, Rosie wondered what her child would taste like.

Bio-Gulag

John Maddox's subconscious was aware of the gradual temperature drop on his naked skin long before his brain functions returned. His blood, thinned by regular doses of anticoagulant, slowly withdrew from his skin's surface, thus retaining valuable body heat. His liver began to spasm, sporadically at first, like an old car engine spluttering to life after years of neglect, his core muscles picking up the beat. Soon John was shivering in response to the steadily cooling fluid surrounding him.

The thick, ribbed tube, previously feeding a constant supply of anaesthetic gases into his lungs, now began providing an oxygen-rich air mixture instead. As the gases cleared John's bloodstream the oxygen level automatically reduced until, almost an hour after the process had begun, he was breathing a standard air mixture. The computer monitoring his condition recorded an elapsed time of thirty-two minutes between the re-establishment of normal respiratory function and his eyes flickering open.

It was dark. A small red light drifted across his eye-line, but John didn't know whether it was real or just his brain playing tricks. His body floated gently in a viscous hypotonic solution, effectively cocooning him from the outside world. His head felt congested, plus his temples were pounding, making it hard to focus. John had no recollection of his life before the fluid and certainly no understanding of how he'd become immersed; he'd only had the dreams. Vivid and terrifying, the drug-fuelled hallucinations were capable of twisting a man's mind until he willingly accepted madness as a blessed relief.

John tentatively stretched his hand into the darkness enveloping him. He wasn't sure if he was awake; was this darkness real or imagined? And what lurked out there, beyond his reach and sight? His fingertips brushed against something smooth. Instinctively his hand recoiled, the pounding in his head increasing to a frenzy as his blood-pressure spiked. Unknown to John, the electronic brain administered a vaso-dilator, correcting the temporary imbalance created by the shock, meaning his blood pressure quickly returned to normal. As the pounding receded, he overcame a moment of indecision and pushed out his hand again.

This time, when his hand pressed against the unnaturally cold surface, John was braver. The surface was smooth to touch but solid. He tried to swivel round with awkward, clumsy movements, but his limbs, weakened by inactivity, just flailed helplessly in the dense fluid. Suspended in the utter darkness, he couldn't even be sure he was floating in a vertical position; the pressure behind his eyeballs might just be a result of floating head down, but without a reference point he couldn't tell.

John abandoned his attempts to move, instead allowing his body to float in the womb of the darkness. If there was someone there with him, he wasn't able to touch, or talk to them. Seconds passed with interminal slowness, the minutes stretching into hours, and all the while he was alone with his jumbled thoughts.

Then, with the flick of a distant switch, John was bathed in a blinding brilliance. Lights fitted into the ends of the glass cylinder in which John found himself, shone into the fluid. The intensity burned his eyes, and even when he screwed them tightly shut, spectral images danced across the back of his eyelids. He waited for them to fade before carefully opening his eyes. He peered into the pitch black beyond the glass confines, just about making out dark figures lurking in the shadows. Straining his eyes against the sticky fluid, he tried to focus on one of them, hoping it would trigger a memory.

A grotesquely distorted face appeared on the other side of the glass. The curvature of the tube pulled the features into a misshapen image while the yellow light cast bizarre shadow patterns across its skin. The face stared at John for a few seconds before disappearing back into the darkness. John frantically shouted for help, but the tube in his throat prevented him from forming words or even uttering sounds, leaving him staring silently out of his glass prison.

A loud clunking sound, the volume amplified by the liquid, resonated up through the cylinder, a thin stream of tiny bubbles sparkled as they caught the powerful beams. The fluid below John churned, a small vortex forming beneath his feet. Despite its size, he was aware of its power as it dragged at his legs, pulling him down towards the bright circle of light.

With a loud roar in his ears, John's head broke the surface. The sticky fluid plastered his long hair to his head, the matted strands stuck across his face. The air was colder than the receding liquid and, without anything to support his body, John slumped helplessly against the pod's Perspex side. His face slid down the cool smoothness until he finally came to rest in a quivering heap on the perforated metal plate at the foot of his clear cell. A soft hydraulic hiss was followed by a cloud of condensation, frosting the pod's sides and obscuring what little vision John had.

Unable to stop himself from toppling forward, John fell to the floor, the tube tugging painfully at his throat. Strong hands pulled roughly at him, flipping him face-up before sliding the tube free. His lungs burned as he sucked in cool air, then convulsed violently, sending mouthfuls of thick liquid and acidic bile spewing across his chest. The unseen hands rolled him over and thick rubbery fingers forced their way inside his mouth, clearing away the vomit before a cold wet cloth wiped him clean.

It took John several minutes to get the wracking cough under control, the exertion tiring his already frail body. When shadowy figures dragged him from the floor and onto an uncomfortable steel gurney, he couldn't offer any resistance. He tried peeking at the people around him, but couldn't focus his sore, half-closed eyes, even in the still dark room. He could only make out shadows and outlines as they wheeled him through a set of double doors and down an equally badly lit corridor. John couldn't fight it any longer, so he closed his eyes, letting exhaustion wash over him.

John awoke lying on his back under a thin white sheet, the light above him, although not bright, stinging his eyes. He tried lifting his arm to shield his face, but discovered his forearm securely strapped to the gurney's metal frame. Glancing down, he noticed a bandage on his wrist with several brightly coloured intravenous ports protruding from its outer folds. While a couple lay unused, one was connected to a syringe pump next to the gurney, the soft humming and luminous screen telling him it was working.

From beyond his field of vision John heard something being moved, followed by heavy footsteps.

"Good morning. I trust you slept well?" The voice came from his left and John strained his neck to look for its source, but to no avail. The voice continued with a hollow chuckle, "Of course you didn't, those dreams are horrific aren't they? Some get really weird; I mean total head fuck stuff. That's why the medical boards don't approve that particular anaesthetic's use; it has side effects that are detrimental to a patient's mental state. But for us... well, let's just say it has cost advantages. The nightmares are just an added bonus as far as we're concerned."

John opened his mouth to speak. He needed answers to questions, such as; where was he and why was he here? And more importantly, who was he? He still had no memory of anything before the dreams, and even those were growing distant. But the words stuck in his parched throat, the only sound to leave his mouth was a stifled croak.

"I wouldn't try to speak yet; it usually takes about a week for your voice to return." A ghostly image passed briefly through John's peripheral vision. The voice added, "I will arrange for food and water to be brought to you and then we'll get you cleaned up." He heard a door open and close; John was alone again.

How long had he been lying here? An hour? Perhaps longer? Time had lost all meaning, John's mind trapped inside a weak useless shell, his senses deprived of the vital stimuli connecting his mind to the outside world. He feared he would go crazy. Maybe he already had. Perhaps this was a reality created by his insanity, his memory erased by madness. The sound of the door opening interrupted his desperate search for rationality, something he could hold onto. Powerful lights hummed into life above him, their intensity boring through his closed eyelids and searing swirling patterns of light deep into his head.

He felt the bed moving, tilting him upright until he was lying almost vertically. The plastic ties securing his wrists and ankles to the bed bit deeply into his skin as he slid down, his weight held by their thin strapping. When he was released, without warning, his exhausted body fell limply to the floor. Hands, gentler than before, helped him onto wobbly legs and guided him to a small chair.

He peered at the young woman preparing his breakfast. A mask covered her nose and mouth, but John could see her eyes. They were cold and distant, detached from the job at hand. She made no attempt to talk to him, but simply went about her duty with a calm efficient manner. Only once she'd placed the bowl and plastic spoon on the table in front of him did she make eye-contact. It was brief, almost accidental, but she quickly looked away before hurriedly leaving the room. In that brief instant, John had seen fear; the basic raw fear an animal shows when faced with a deadly predator, and the fear had been directed at him.

He looked down at the contents of the bowl. It was sloppy, odourless and looked revolting, even to John's starved palate. He fumbled with the spoon; his fine motor skills hadn't yet returned sufficiently, making it harder than it should have been. He quickly abandoned the spoon and used his fingers instead, bending his head forward and shovelling the slop directly into his mouth. He realised his visual assessment of the food's quality was vastly inaccurate; the slop was absolutely vile. He resisted the urge to spit it out. He was weak and hungry and, vile or not, it was still food.

John sat there eating for a long time. Initially, he felt inclined to vomit after each mouthful, but soon became too tired to even notice how disgusting the food tasted. He finally fell asleep, his face lying on the slop-covered table. He was oblivious to the masked woman's return and to the injection she administered. Neither did he stir after she was joined by several other similarly masked figures, who lifted him back onto his gurney and re-secured his wrists.

"Wake up, John." It was the same voice as before. Somehow it was reaching into his dreams and guiding him back to consciousness. He opened his eyes, then immediately closed them again. Bright overhead lights blazed down on him. "I'm sorry about the lights, but it's an unfortunate necessity, I'm afraid." The disembodied voice moved around him, John heard the soft clicking of shoes as whoever it was, walked. "I hope the food was satisfactory. Our chefs are not particular skilled at gourmet food, but they do know their slop."

John struggled to lift his head so he could turn it in the direction of the voice. Through one eye he made out a dark-suited figure standing with his back to the gurney on which he was still lying. The man nodded to someone behind John's head, "Sit him up, please."

Despite the politeness of the request, John was left in no doubt about the stranger's authority. The soft whirring of an electric motor came from below the gurney and his upper body began to rise until he was at a forty-five degree angle. Dark Suit nodded and John's ascent came to an abrupt halt.

His eyes were gradually becoming accustomed to the glare so he took the opportunity to look around the room. It was large, but sparsely furnished, if furniture was the right word for a metal table, two matching chairs, and a wheeled trolley containing several drawers. Apart from his gurney, John couldn't see any other furnishings. The walls were a drab pale green and three of them were completely bare, the fourth dominated by a large black glass window.

Images flashed across John's mind. Masked figures laughed as they sliced through his flesh, tearing the organs from his body. Blood, so much blood, cascading from his open stomach cavity, flowing over the gurney and onto the floor, forming a deep red pool in which the figures paddled and laughed hysterically at each new organ they pulled from his body. And watching from the window was the faceless Dark Suit.

John fought against the restraints pulling at his arms. His breath came in shallow gasps, the air making rasping sounds as it escaped through tense vocal chords. Fear and exertion stimulated his adrenal glands, causing his heart to race. His rising body temperature caused a soft sheen to form on his skin as he struggled to escape the evocative reality of his own mind.

"Ah! I think our guest's memory may be returning." Dark Suit now stood directly over him, his features obscured by a mask. Deep lines etching his forehead betrayed his advancing years, yet his deep blue eyes burned with the intensity and passion of youth.

"Welcome back, John Maddox. I hope you don't mind, but to expedite events we took the liberty of conducting our tests while you slept. There is a pressing need to conclude affairs quicker than usual." The suited stranger pointed towards the black window, "Your results are displayed there." As he spoke, a series of numbers and body scan images appeared on the glass. "I'm sure they make no sense at all to you, so let me summarise the salient points. You are remarkably healthy, all things considered. Your respiratory and cardiac functions have returned to within normal range and blood tests show your renal and hepatic functions are good. The brain scan shows cell damage to be well within acceptable levels, while the bio-scan shows no sign of illness or infection. So we are happy to proceed."

The stranger had started to walk away, but, almost as an afterthought, he turned back to John, "I'm sure you have many questions. Your memory will be fully restored at the appropriate time and this will undoubtedly provide you with many of the answers you seek. Good day."

Then he was gone, the steady click of his shoes receding into the distance as the gurney whirred into life, lowering his head until he was once more lying flat. The lights around the room dimmed, all except a bank of lights directly above him, which continued to burn down on his near-naked body.

Another masked figure, John thought it may have been the young woman who had brought his food, appeared and, without saying a word, pushed a syringe into his flank just above the hip. She then busied herself laying instruments out on a couple of trollies, which she brought to the side of the gurney just as a second figure appeared. They too wore a mask. The second figure looked down at John dispassionately before reaching for the instruments on the nearest trolley. He — John felt sure it was a man — produced a scalpel and, without explanation, made a long arching incision around John's flank.

The expected pain never arrived. Paralysed, John could only watch as the two masked figures operated on his prostrate body, his horrific dreams coming to life before his eyes. Had they been premonitions, or had he endured this torture before?

The two worked in almost total silence with only the occasional whispered conversation passing between them. John could only observe as they continued cutting through layers of fat and muscle. Once finished, they shoved their hands into the open chasm they'd created. He felt fingers tugging at his insides, felt them pushing his internal organs around. He watched as they lifted his kidney free, holding it up for inspection before dismissively placing it in a plastic kidney dish.

John felt a rising tide of terror. It started in his chest, a tight ball rising into his throat, gathering momentum until it engulfed every fibre of his being. Unable to move and powerless to prevent them looting his body, his mind panicked, his thoughts raced. How many organs were they taking? Was he to die here, without knowing why? Not even knowing who he was?

The surgeon picked up a Petri dish containing a tiny sample of tissue. He carefully removed it with tweezers before inserting it into John's open body cavity. His assistant handed him a suture needle with which he stitched the sample into the space from where he'd removed the kidney. John watched as the two figures completed their work and closed the incision, carefully sewing along the wound and pulling the edges together. Once closed, they applied a sticky paste over the wound. John was held in a shocked trance, divorced from the proceedings, as though the events were happening to someone else.

Once they'd finished the operation, the surgeons left the instruments on the trolley and walked from the room. John lay on his back, unable to move. His side felt uncomfortable and sore, but he wasn't in pain. John also felt he wasn't alone, so he waited — there was nothing else he could do. Eventually the familiar voice of Dark Suit broke the silence.

"See, John, that was all quite painless," said the man, his shoes clicking in time to the rhythm of his voice. "I expect you would like to see the surgeon's handiwork. After all, it *is* your body." The voice broke into a soft, but deep laugh, adding, "Sorry, private joke. It's not your body, it's ours, has been for a long time, since before I started working here, in fact." He clicked his fingers and the lights above John's gurney slid away to reveal a long mirror.

John stared at the naked image. For the first time since he'd awoken in the cylindrical tank he saw his own face. It was the face of a stranger. He looked young, he was clean-shaven and his eyes were strong, even defiant. The sticky paste applied by the surgeon had dried, creating a flexible skin-like material which blended in with his natural tone, making the incision line almost invisible. His body looked pale and bloated, with little muscle definition but then, John couldn't remember if he'd ever been muscular in the first place.

John felt awkward, almost voyeuristic, staring at his unrecognisable naked body. Then he looked away, acutely aware of his own vulnerability. It wasn't being strapped to the gurney, he'd got used to that, nor was it the chemically induced feeling of weirdness. Neither of those helped, but it was his own nudity which really made him feel... exposed.

Hearing Dark Suit laughing only made the feelings worse. "Not a pretty sight, is it John? Think yourself lucky, I've had to look at your ugly bloated body every time I inspected the holding tanks." Another finger click and the lights were extinguished, leaving John shrouded in darkness again. He heard Dark Suit's footsteps fading away, followed by a brief shaft of light as a door opens and is then slammed shut.

Again, John was alone in darkness. For a while he fought to remain awake, but finally succumbed to the inevitable rising tide of sleep. He felt the warmth of an evening sun on his face, cool water gently lapping against his tired feet. He felt the power of the waves as water rose to his waist and lifted him off his feet. Stretching out an arm to steady himself, he struck a smooth cold surface and his eyes snapped open. The setting sun was gone, replaced by a solitary light shining directly into his face as the rising water rapidly refilled his glass pod.

John tried to scream, but the thick tube was back in his throat. He slapped frantically against the reinforced glass, the water rising past his nipples, the rational part of his mind panicking as the liquid reached his face. He tilted his head back as the viscous substance swirled around his neck while his feet were lifted clear of the metal plate. He could just make out the pod's ceiling as the oily, slimy fluid engulfed him and anaesthetic gases pumped into his lungs. His eyes closed and his arms floated gently down by his sides as he drifted into unconsciousness, suspended in liquid incarceration.

Standing behind the solitary bright light, the dark-suited official of the Bio Correction Department opened his file and took a few steps forward until he was standing face-to-face with John. He took a moment to acquaint himself with the details, then read aloud.

"John Maddox. You were sentenced by the Court of Freedom and Liberty for crimes against an individual. The sentence decrees you should remain in a designated detention facility until you have provided no less than six harvests."

Anxious to get the details correct, the man paused for a brief moment to check the notes. He flicked through a few pages, then continued, "Today you provided harvest five, specifically a kidney. You were also implanted with a synthetic bio-seed which will be harvested when fully developed. You will now be returned to your suspended state until you are required again." He gently patted the glass tank, "By the way, your daughter died a few years ago. She was seventy-two, I think." Staring in at John's face, he shrugged. "I'll see you in about twenty years, Mr Maddox."

As the official left the room, the light flicked out and the camera recording the incident for John's memory, switched off and transferred the file to a Central Storage Unit. In the darkness, Prisoner 6879 Maddox was left alone to face the grotesque demons haunting his dreams.

A Zombie Is For Christmas, Not The Afterlife

Like most teenage boys, Stephen had left his Christmas shopping until absolutely the last moment. While his sister Beth enjoyed a Christmas Eve visit to Santa's grotto, followed by a burger in one of the fast-food outlets scattered around the mall, he trudged from store to store, searching for inspiration.

Finally settling on an art set for his sister, an ugly dog ornament his mum would go embarrassingly crazy over and aftershave smelling suspiciously like bottled cat piss for his father, he hurried to meet the others. Cutting through the crowds of last-minute shoppers and heading for their prearranged meeting point at the fountain, he passed little stalls selling a large array of Christmas items. Stopping at one to buy wrapping paper and a packet of small gift tags, he noticed the neighbouring stall was selling an enticing array of sweets and treats. The air had a spicy seasonal aroma, a mix of cinnamon, nutmeg and roasted chestnuts. Fighting the urge to buy a toffee-apple, Stephen moved on, not wanting to keep his mother waiting.

Taking a hasty shortcut through a department store, he sidestepped an old couple sauntering in the other direction, but then crashed headfirst into one of the shop's mannequins. It rocked backwards, toppling over. Instinctively, Stephen dropped his shopping bags and reached out to grab it, but he was too late. The life-size plastic doll hit the ground with a loud crash and Stephen, his feet becoming entwined in the mannequin's legs, followed it.

Sprawled as he was across the dummy while trying to untangle himself, Stephen was aware that he could possible look like some deviant with a plastic fetish. Red-faced, he got back to his feet just in time to see a severe-looking sales assistant coming towards him, cutting through the crowds like a war galleon in full sail. Grabbing his shopping, Stephen made a hasty exit, the assistant's accusations of "Vandal" and "Hooligan," and helpful advice like, "Look where you're going next time!" ringing in his ears. Heading for one of the store's exits, he prayed the assistant hadn't alerted security and they weren't about to seize him so close to freedom.

He stepped out onto the main plaza close to the fountain, relieved to see his mum and sister waiting by the giant Christmas tree. He hurried towards them not wanting to spend any longer than necessary in the mall.

"There you are. Did you get everything you needed?" His mother didn't wait for his answer before continuing, "You look flushed. Is everything okay?"

Nodding, Stephen lifted his bags slightly to indicate his purchases and muttered, "Yeah, fine. I've been running that's all." He started wandering towards the lifts and escalators leading to the car park, signalling his willingness to go home.

Beth smiled at her brother, "He wants to get home so he can ring Amanda," dragging out each syllable of the name so it took three times as long to say, while theatrically clutching her heart.

"Ha. Ha. Ha." Stephen replied, sneering at his sister.

"I'm pretty sure you mean 'Ho. Ho. Ho." Beth broke out into a fit of giggles, ducking away from Stephen as he took a swing at her with the wrapping paper.

"Will you two stop it?" The look on their mother's face told the siblings it was a rhetorical question best left unanswered. Having glared at them for long enough to get her point across, she gathered her bags and headed for the lift with her two chastened offspring following.

Ten minutes later she was guiding the car through snow-covered streets and out into the queue of holiday traffic towards the suburbs. Stephen sat in the front, his fight with Beth forgotten. They spent the whole journey exchanging small talk, excitedly pointing out brightly-lit houses decked out with festive decorations or an inflatable Santa Clause bobbing on a roof, but it wasn't long before they were pulling into their driveway.

Wasting no time, Stephen jumped out of the car almost before his mum had applied the hand-brake and rushed into the house. Stopping briefly in the kitchen to steal a mince pie, he charged upstairs to wrap his recently bought presents. Laying the gifts out on his bed, he was halfway through the wrapping when he heard the doorbell chime. Hearing his father direct the caller to leave whatever it was in the garage, he moved to the window that overlooked the street. All he saw was a plain truck parked at the end of the drive, its hazard lights flashing brightly in the late afternoon gloom. Then two men wearing overalls walked out of the garage and down the driveway, before getting into the truck and driving away. Shrugging, he returned to his task, but before he could pick up the sticky tape, his father called up to him.

"Stephen, can you come downstairs for a minute? I need a hand with something."

Cursing under his breath, Stephen shouted back, "Sure, Dad. I'll be right down." Hiding the unwrapped presents in a cupboard, he went downstairs, knowing that whatever his father needed a hand with was going to take far longer than a minute. He and his sister had only been living with their adoptive parents for a little-over two years, but they'd been virtual servants since the adoption woman had left the house.

Walking into the kitchen, he found mother reading a gossip magazine while Beth was preparing vegetables.

"Where's Dad?" He had long ago learnt to keep the irritation out of his voice. His mother didn't even answer him, instead pointing towards the door to the garage and workshop area.

Walking into the freezing garage almost took his breath away. He felt the cold rush in through his mouth and nose and down into his chest, making his lungs tighten as if frozen. Small clouds of vapour danced from his lips as he exhaled warm air in preparation for another icy blast. The second breath wasn't anywhere near as bad as the first, with the tightness in his chest beginning to ease. Looking around, he saw Dad standing next to a large crate near the front of the garage, a childish grin spread across his features. From experience, Stephen knew that look meant trouble.

"Ta-dah!" he said, making a grand sweeping gesture towards the wooden box.

Looking at it, then back at his Dad grinning inanely, Stephen sighed, "Okay, just because it's Christmas I'm going to be polite and pretend I'm interested in your crate."

"Take a closer look, Stephen. Read what it says on the lid." His Dad now looked like a child in a candy store.

Walking up to it, Stephen noticed the crate was constructed of wood screwed onto a sturdy metal frame. Stencilled onto the lid was the supplier's name and logo. A clear plastic wallet containing a shipping address and a booklet marked, - *INSTRUCTIONS* - were stuck securely to the wood using yellow tape with - *EXTREME CARE: BIOHAZARD* – repeatedly printed in thick black lettering. Stephen let the pieces sort themselves out in his head; when he was sure, he read it again, out loud this time.

"The Dead Helpful Company," he said, not sure whether he was saying it to his father or himself. He looked at his father who was now nodding so violently Stephen thought his head was about to fall off. "You bought a zombie for Christmas. How fuckin' cool!"

"Watch your mouth!" His father didn't stop smiling or nodding, "Uncle Richard is on his way over to help get it set up so we can have it working tonight."

"Oh great, Uncle Dick's coming." Stephen liked to emphasise the name to make his feelings about his adoptive uncle clear. He and Beth liked Uncle Richard even less than their adoptive parents. He had no sense of responsibility and generally acted like a complete idiot, especially when drunk. *And* it was Christmas Eve.

Ignoring Stephen's barbed comment, his dad took a powered screwdriver from a toolbox. Standing over the eight-feet long crate, he began undoing the series of screws securing the lid. Stephen remained standing, silently watching as each screw was removed, his anticipation rising as each one fell to the floor. After the first five had been removed he began shifting his weight from foot to foot, impatience gnawing at him. As the seventh screw bounced onto the concrete, his frustration burst. Reaching into the toolbox he picked out a retractable knife, using it to cut open the plastic wallet.

Placing the shipping note to one side, Stephen read the instruction manual. Skipping through the usual blurb congratulating the purchaser on their decision to buy this model, he came to the page explaining the installation and setup process. "We need to follow this set of instructions," he said, waving the booklet at his father who was busy undoing the last screw. Letting it fall, the older man straightened up, the huge inane grin returning. Sitting down wearily on the crate, he gestured for his son to join him.

Sitting down awkwardly, Stephen offered the booklet to his father, but he waved it away. "You read it, son. Then we'll crack this cadaver's coffin open and let him tidy up. Why buy a zombie and moan yourself?" He laughed at his own joke, but Stephen just looked away, shuddering inwardly at the use of the term – *son*. As soon as they were able to, he and Beth were going to leave, to find somewhere of their own to live, away from this evil couple with their thin veil of respectability.

Clearing his throat, Stephen read aloud. "*Dead Helpful* cannot accept responsibility for any damage to property or loss of life, either directly or indirectly, caused by the buyer's or operator's failure to comply with the guidelines and instructions set out in this manual."

"Yeah, yeah. Let's get to the important part."

Just as Stephen was about to continue, Uncle Richard entered the garage through the door from the main house. He was wearing a set of flashing antlers and a long scarf with large woollen snowballs on each end. "Wow! It's cold in here. Is that so the stiff thinks he's still in the mortuary?" He removed the antlers and turned them off, putting them in his coat pocket.

"No, it's 'cos it's the middle of winter and snowing," Stephen sneered, making sure Richard knew he thought him stupid.

Richard looked at Stephen, his lip curled, and then laughed aloud, "Little Stevie has mastered sarcasm. I'm so proud." He leant closer to Stephen, ruffling his hair. Annoyed, Stephen pulled away and smoothed his hair back into place.

"Stephen is just about to read out the instructions for getting this baby up and running," announced Stephen's adopted parent, high-fiving his brother.

"Wow! Little Stevie can read," said Richard, a look of mock surprise on his face.

His uncle was acting like a real idiot. Stephen skimmed through the opening paragraph while ignoring him and trying not to let the comments rile him. He knew if he did he was letting these bullies win, and if he overstepped the mark he would be punished for his insolence. Clearing his throat, Stephen summarised what he'd read. "Okay, the crate contains not only the zombie, although they prefer to call them 'reclaimed bodies,' but also the clothes you originally ordered. They're also provided with a generic white boiler suit for general day-to-day wear."

"There's a huge range of costumes and accessories in the catalogue, some of it quite disturbing. I mean, who would want their zombie to look like Rob Patterson complete with 'Team Edward' T-shirt?" Stephen's father said looking genuinely perplexed.

Richard shook his head in disbelief, "There are some sick, sick people out there. What next? Zombie Ken and Barbie complete with pink sports car and interchangeable heads." Even Stephen recognised the humour of the situation with an involuntary snigger. Richard laughed harder, appearing to remember some private joke. Pointing his finger in the air as a signal for the other two to listen, he began recounting his tale. "One Christmas, when we were kids, your dad and I ripped the head off your Aunt's doll and stuck a dinosaur's head on it. Then we tried selling it back to her as 'reptile Barbie'. She went completely ape-shit, it was fucking hilarious."

This time, Stephen refused to join in the two men's raucous laughter, thinking them spiteful and immature. The only member of his adoptive inbreeds who ever showed any real kindness to him and his sister was Aunt Eve, and Stephen genuinely liked her.

After waiting a short while for the laughter to subside, he continued, "The crate also contains a care pack containing a supply of everything we'll need to maintain the reclaimed... zombie." He quickly read on. "Okay, I get it now. Inside the care pack there's a smaller box containing a set of prefilled syringes, a year's supply of what they refer to as 'appetite suppressants,' which are patches you attach to the zombie's skin."

While Stephen was talking, the two older men stood on either side of him and, without warning, lifted the crate lid up, tipping him on the floor. Jumping back to his feet, he joined the men in staring into the open crate. It took them a moment or two to comprehend fully the sight before them. Finally, Richard said, "It's a bit on the blue side."

Stephen spent a few more seconds studying the dead man lying in the box. Only his front was visible, the rest of him encased in moulded polystyrene. The back of the discarded lid also contained a moulding, ensuring all-round protection during transit. The cadaver's closed eyes gave him a surreal peaceful appearance. Wedging his mouth slightly open was a small red stopper. The body was completely naked. Its pale skin did indeed have a blue tinge to it, especially around the mouth and extremities. White plastic strapping secured his ankles, wrists and neck in place.

A clear plastic box had been placed in the space between the tall, well-built man's feet, Stephen's father crouched and quickly removed the box, as if doing so might awaken the beast. Under that was a second, larger cardboard box, which Richard removed with an equal amount of false bravado.

Standing up, Stephen's dad said, with a nod towards the dead man's genitals, "I thought it would come wearing something, maybe the white boiler suit or a loincloth."

Richard pointed at the cadaver's groin, "Don't let your Clair see that, otherwise you may be the one sleeping in a crate in the garage." Stephen was trying hard not to laugh, aware he might get a beating if he did. His father gave a sarcastic laugh in Richard's direction, but his eyes betrayed him by displaying real mirth. Something Stephen rarely saw from this soulless bully unless he was punishing either him or his sister.

Stephen returned to the manual he'd dropped after they'd tipped him off the crate. "The care pack also contains a special moisturizer designed to stop the skin drying out and to slow down the decomposition process." As Stephen read this out his father opened the plastic box and began laying its contents out on the work surface.

"What's that for?" Richard pointed. Inside the crate's lid was a long handled fire axe strapped onto the polystyrene.

Flicking over a page in the manual, Stephen continued to read silently for a few seconds then looked directly at Richard.

"Emergencies."

All three stared in silence at the inert zombie, suddenly aware of its lethal instincts.

"That's cool," said Richard, picking up a knife. He cut the axe free from the polystyrene, took up a baseball stance and attempted a few practice swings. Nodding his approval of the tool's craftsmanship, he placed it carefully on the workbench.

Having finished laying out the contents of the care box, Stephen's father tossed it onto the workbench next to the axe. Richard pointed to the container with the syringes and asked, "I know I'm gonna regret asking this, but what do we do with those?" He looked expectantly at Stephen as he finished his question.

The box contained six blue vials and one bright green one, each having a snub nose with a screw thread connection and a red plastic guard covering the plunger. Stephen didn't need to consult the manual.

"The green one kick-starts metabolic activity, a bit like an un-dead Red Bull. The blue ones act as a preservative and you inject one every eight weeks. There's a special port embedded in the skin on the back of his neck that only approved syringes attach to."

Picking up the small packet of patches, Richard studied them intently. Looking puzzled, he asked, "These appetite suppressing patches, what appetite does a zombie have that needs suppressing? They're dead... undead... stiffs... whatever you call them."

Stephen looked at his uncle for a moment, a look of disbelief on his face. Speaking with a deliberately patronising tone he said, "Well I'm no expert, but, as I understand it, they are partial to feasting on human brains." Then, unable to resist it any longer, even if it meant getting a beating, he added, "Although, I suspect, if they cracked your skull they'll be sadly disappointed." He flinched as his adoptive loser of a father raised his hand, but the expected punch didn't arrive. When he looked up, he saw the hand waiting for a high-five. Cautiously he slapped his palm to his father's open hand.

Smiling, Richard said, "All right smartass, I guess I deserved that. So what do we do now?"

Stephen continued to read through the instructions, making sure he fully understood what they had to do. He was aware of the trust placed in him with such an important job and he needed to make absolutely sure he got it right. The consequences of making a mistake were almost too horrific to contemplate.

While Stephen was busy reading, Richard opened the cardboard box he'd removed from the crate earlier. Smiling, he took out a Santa suit complete with black boots and a matching belt. "Is this what you couldn't tell me about on the phone, 'cos Claire and Beth were listening?"

"Yeah, I thought it might be an amusing surprise for them. It's not often that you can get Santa to deliver presents to your room on Christmas

Morning," his brother replied.

"It's not often a kid wakes up to find a skinny blue stiff roaming around her bedroom in the middle of the night, masquerading as Santa Clause. You're going to scare the living crap out of 'em." Richard, for once, had his serious face on.

"Yeah, when you put it as succinctly as that, you do have a point. I didn't really think the whole costume thing through. I'll order a more sensible set of clothes after Christmas." Stephen's father took the Santa suit from his brother and folded it up.

Shaking his head, Richard replied, "I think that would be a wise move."

Taking his chance to cut in on the conversation Stephen spoke again, regaining the two older men's attention. "Right, here we go." Stephen placed the open manual down on the bench.

"First, we need to completely unpack the zombie. Apparently the crate comes apart to make this easier." He stood watching, occasionally trying to offer helpful advice as the pair struggled to free the zombie from its polystyrene mould. Finally the body was wrestled free and put face up on the cold floor.

"There's a tattoo on the left arm," Richard said, peering uncomfortably at the naked man's arm. "It gives his name as 'Christian' and a barcode."

"Maybe that's his religion. So they can dispose of his body correctly." Stephen shrugged, trying to avoid looking at the man's nakedness.

"Nah, they've already had a religious ceremony when they died. The company come and collect the remains at the appropriate time and arrange for their safe disposal," said his dad. "It's a name given to them by Dead Helpful to make them a little more personal. No one knows what their name was during life, it's so their living relatives can't trace them. The barcode is their registration, which means they can be returned to their owners if they're lost or stolen. It also contains their biometric information, meaning we can order clothes and accessories in the correct sizes." Looking at their shocked faces, he added sheepishly, "The representative told me when I rang the dealership to place the order."

"The next item on the agenda is slapping a patch on the back of his neck. This must be done prior to restarting him. According to the manual, they are prone to waking in a ravenous state." Stephen paused, watching Richard carefully peel the backing off one of the patches and then, with his brother's help, roll Christian onto his side. Richard smoothed the patch onto the nape of the dead man's neck before they let him flop back.

"Just like a nicotine patch, and this bad boy's a twenty brains a day corpse," said Richard doing a passable Groucho Marx impression.

"This is a weird feeling," said Stephen. "I've never seen a dead body before and the only zombies I've seen have been at a distance, like those ones they use to fix the roads. Yet here I am, standing in my garage, looking at a dead body and I'm strangely fine with it."

"That's because all you teenagers are total freaks. You're brought up on a diet of sick horror movies and video games," replied Richard, picking up the box of coloured vials. Selecting the single green one, he removed it from the container before handing it to Stephen. "Which is why you have the honour of bringing our new friend, Christian, back to the land of the living, or whatever it is they come back to…?"

Gingerly taking the syringe from his uncle, Stephen looked at his father, seeking confirmation. The man nodded, but backed away slightly. Stephen realised both he and Richard were taking up a position on the other side of the table from the prone zombie.

This was no honour. This was self-preserving cowardice, with him as the sacrificial lamb.

Taking a faltering step towards the inanimate corpse, he realised all he really wanted to do was crap himself. Right there on the garage floor.

Taking a deep breath, he crouched next to Christian's head and slowly stretched out his hand. He was shaking so much he withdrew it again, placing the syringe on the ground next to him. Summoning all the courage he could muster, he shot out his hand before he could change his mind. The flesh was cold and slightly greasy, like a supermarket chicken ready for cooking. He suppressed the urge to turn around and run, he didn't want to give his adoptive father and Uncle Dick the satisfaction of seeing his fear.

Stephen inched his hand round to the back of Christian's neck, his fingers tentatively exploring the cold skin, searching for the small injection port. Locating it, he rolled the heavy head onto its side before picking up the syringe which he, on the third attempt, attached to the port. He took another deep breath, calming his frayed nerves. He felt his heart thumping against the inside of his chest, his breath becoming rapid and shallow. He still had the urge to crap, while his legs had simultaneously taken on the consistency of jelly and the mobility of stone.

Snapping the red safety guard off, he tried telling himself that people re-animated zombies every day of the week and lived to tell the tale. The law of averages was on his side. But that was other people. Applying the theory of relativity and the laws of probability to his situation, Stephen was relatively sure he was probably going to die.

Taking a quick glance towards the two men hiding behind the workbench, Stephen pressed the plunger, forcing the bright green fluid into the port and on into the zombie's neck.

Having emptied the syringe, he shuffled backwards across the floor, never taking his eyes off the motionless cadaver. The three of them watched, transfixed, as the zombie known as Christian did... absolutely nothing. No involuntary twitching of muscle, no moaning sigh signalling his return to life, no ravening rampage of murderous mayhem.

He just lay on the cold floor, motionless.

After a whole minute of the corpse doing nothing, Richard's patience ran out, "Well that was an anti-climax." Pointing at the discarded manual he said, "What does the holy book say about this?" Although his comment didn't appear to be aimed at anyone specific, Stephen recovered the manual and began reading the section marked *Trouble-shooting*. Meanwhile, Richard was creeping towards Christian, his courage buoyed by the lack of movement exhibited by him. Finally, standing above their dead guest, he bent over, peering into the lifeless features.

Christian opened his eyes.

Letting out the sort of scream usually heard from heroines in old black and white movies, Richard scampered out of the zombies reach and hid behind the workbench. Christian didn't take any notice of the fleeing man. He simply started climbing unsteadily to his feet with deliberate yet uncoordinated movements, until eventually he stood upright. Swaying slightly from side to side, he flexed his fingers and rolled his shoulders as if discovering them for the first time.

Looking at the walking dead man with a combination of gut-wrenching terror and childish curiosity, Stephen noticed the eyes first. They'd shrunken back into the skull and showed no emotion, no spark of life. If the eyes were the windows of the soul, then Christian's were Hell's viewing gallery. Stephen didn't know what he had been expecting, but he sure as hell knew this wasn't it.

Hearing his dad's voice, he forced himself to tear his eyes away from the shuffling wreck of what was once a human being. His father, retrieving the Santa suit from the workbench, threw it on the floor in front of Christian.

No, not Christian. He threw it in front of the zombie. Stephen realised giving this shambolic marionette a name was abhorrent. No amount of names or fancy costumes could ever make this human again. Stephen had once thought owning a zombie would be cool. Now he knew it was just inhumane.

His dad was speaking directly to the zombie. "Christian, could you get dressed in those clothes on the floor in front of you." Watching the zombie struggle to pick up the bright red tunic and fumble with the belt obviously amused both him and Richard. When he became entangled in the trousers and fell flat on his face, the pair of them laughed as if watching a Charlie Chaplin slapstick routine.

"Do you not think this is just a little disturbing?" asked Richard. Stephen looked at his uncle, hopeful that common sense was about to prevail, that his annoying relative was about to stop this macabre charade. But then Richard continued, "Us three standing in a garage watching a naked guy play dress up?"

Watching these tormentors laugh at the vulnerable zombie trying to get dressed in that ridiculous suit, complete with bushy white beard, was too much for Stephen to bear. He turned away and finished reading the instruction booklet, taking careful note of the back page. After a while, the zombie finally finished getting dressed. Looking around the untidy garage, Stephen's dad said, "Richard, give me a hand to sort this place out. Put the vials and patches back in the box and get Christian to tidy this mess." He nodded towards the packing materials scattered across the floor. "Stephen, you can run off like a good boy and get your mother's presents from my study." He looked directly at Stephen before adding in a menacing tone, "And no snooping around in there."

The two men turned their attention to the dismantled crate and polystyrene packaging littering the floor. While they were busy carefully repacking the preservation fluids and syringes into the plastic box, Stephen casually wandered past the workbench, picking up the axe. The bewildered zombie was standing at the end of the bench, watching him with his soulless eyes as if waiting his instructions. Walking with a newfound purpose, Stephen moved behind the zombie and, in one swift movement, tore the patch away from the nape of his neck.

This will teach them to laugh at him, to beat him, to threaten him, to hurt his sister. He hurried through the door and into the warm welcoming house, bolting it behind him. He remained by the door until the screaming stopped. Then, picking up the axe, he went in search of his dear mother.

He found her sitting at the kitchen table, sorting the linen for Christmas dinner. Without looking up she asked, "Have you boys finished screaming and hollering out there? It's enough to wake the dead."

"Yes, mother, we have. But you won't have to worry about the dead waking up anymore." Swinging the axe handle down onto her unprotected skull, he caught her completely by surprise, splitting the back of her head open. She slumped forward, blood splattering across the white tablecloth. He'd considered using the axe blade, but didn't want to make a mess. Not that he cared about the linen, but he needed his mother's body as undamaged as possible.

Picking up a mince pie, he returned to the garage door and put his ear to the wood. Listening intently for a few moments, he could hear nothing except his own racing heartbeat. Taking a deep breath, he quietly slid the bolt back and pushed the door inwards. There was no sign of either the two men or the zombie. Stealing himself, he renewed his grip on the axe and stepped over the threshold into the cold December air of the garage.

As he moved cautiously into the room, searching the darker edges for signs of movement, Stephen's foot stepped on something soft and yielding. He froze, too scared to look down, and too scared not too. Stealing a quick glance, Stephen lifted his foot. It was Richard's remains.

His bottom jaw had been ripped away and his left arm detached at the elbow, leaving a ragged stump of mangled flesh. But the rest of his scarred and broken body lay face up under Stephen's foot. A large pool of dark blood spread outwards from his severed jaw. Stephen could smell its coppery odour. Richard's dead eyes stared accusingly at the boy as he stepped over him and past the wooden packing crate.

Hearing a strange sound from the far end of the garage, behind the workbench, Stephen crept slowly onwards. Gripping the axe in both hands, he edged around the end of the workbench. In the far corner, he spotted his dad's legs protruding from behind a large rolling toolbox. They were motionless. Taking a step to the side, he saw the zombie sitting astride the man's torso. The strange sound he heard was the tearing of exposed brain from the skull.

Taking another step forward, Stephen raised the axe. Zombie Santa looked up, his grey beard streaked with shades of red and brown as new blood mingled with old. The zombie's eyes were alive now, rejuvenated by the kill. Stephen quickened his pace and swung the axe at Santa's head.

He missed, the axe slamming into the zombie's upper arm, tearing the dead flesh. As Stephen struggled to free it, the zombie started using his other hand to try to wrestle the axe free from his grip. After what felt like an eternity, the axe came loose, allowing Stephen to take another swing, this time severing the head from the shoulders. Complete with fake grey beard, it bounced across the concrete and came to rest against the delivery crate. The body remained kneeling on top of his dad's torso, only falling off when prodded in the chest with the axe.

Taking his father's mobile phone from his pocket and picking up the instruction manual, he flicked to the back page. He reread the advert he'd seen earlier and dialled the number.

After a conversation lasting just a few minutes, Stephen dragged the three bodies into the yard, laying them out side by side in the snow. Returning to the kitchen, he carefully dragged his mother's body out and laid it next to the others. At nearly a hundred thousand for a mostly undamaged body he wanted to cash in. He could claim on *The Dead Helpful Company's* insurance for the accidental death of his family members. The snow would keep them fresh until the company's representative could collect them on Boxing Day.

Closing the garage door, Stephen went to tell Beth the good news.

Dragon Back Falls

Jordan and Steve cruised effortlessly through the early evening crowds thronging the boardwalk. The summer season was drawing to a close and the normally quiet town of Dragon Back was alive with rowdy college kids and arguing families. Occasionally, to maintain their steady speed, the teenagers would smack a foot down on the hot concrete slabs. The skateboard wheels rumbled beneath them as they changed direction with subtle movements.

The massive granite cliffs towering over Dragon Back cast a long shadow over the town. Their saw tooth appearance gave Dragon Back, not only its name, but a sinister reputation, one which was never mentioned in the official guidebooks. Spurned lovers and failed businessmen would come to the town to end their misery by throwing themselves off the high rocky ledges, onto the jagged rocks below.

The two young men rumbled into the darkness of the shadow, heading for the mouth of The Dragon's Lair Funfair, the entrance resembling its namesake's yawning jaws. Jordan could feel a cool breeze on his bare chest as he slid to a stop. Removing his sunglasses, the teen flipped the board up onto its end and caught it with one hand. Steve rolled to a stop next to him, his head bobbing rhythmically in time to the music pumping into his ears from the iPhone tucked into the pocket of his three-quarter length denims.

Jordan pulled on his scruffy Guns 'n' Roses T-shirt as they walked into the reptilian mouth of the Funfair. Hiding their skateboards under the tarpaulin skirting of an ice-cream kiosk, the two of them walked into the swirling chaos of the amusement park.

Although the sun had sunk behind the ridge, the evening was still warm. As the day's shadows lengthened, the fairground lights shone a little brighter. Sirens whooped and howled as rides thundered around their tracks, or hurled screaming, terrified passengers high into the air, only to plunge them back towards earth. Loud rock music played constantly, cranked up until the ground rocked and rolled on a seismic scale. It was this heady atmosphere that attracted so many people to the funfair every night of the summer.

Jordan and Steve had already ridden every ride, played every game of chance, and taken in all the sideshows. They were leaving for college in September and were spending every night of their final Dragon Back summer in The Lair. They knew life would never be the same after this. This was to be their last crazy carefree summer of youth, and they were going to live it to the full.

"I'm hungry! Let's grab something to eat." Steve said, his nose twitching as the smoky tang of hotdog and barbeque sauce wafted past on the gentle breeze.

"Good idea." The aroma of sizzling sausages had caused Jordan's stomach to rumble. He rummaged about in his pocket and produced a few screwed up notes. Selecting one, he stuffed the others back into his pocket and joined his friend at the nearby hotdog stall.

The boys waited patiently while a family argued among themselves over their order. When their turn came Jordan ordered a large hotdog, smothering it in mustard, while Steve picked the excess onion out of his cheeseburger. They ate as they walked through the thronging crowds.

"I'm gonna have another crack at that coconut shy," Steve tried not to let onion fall from his mouth as he spoke. "I've got to win one before summer ends."

Jordan laughed, "No chance of that, mate - you throw like a girl." He staggered sideways as Steve's right arm jabbed into his bicep. "And hit like a baby girl," he added, trying not to show the dull pain that throbbed deep inside his upper arm.

They walked in silence for a few minutes, taking in the sights and sounds of the bustling amusement park. Darkness had driven the last strands of daylight from the sky and now a million multi-coloured lights illuminated the attractions. Lurking between brightly lit concessions and the rides flashing strobe lights stood narrow deeply-shadowed aisles. These dark foreboding gateways led to the fairground's secret underbelly. An underbelly that is alive to the rhythmic beating of a multitude of generators supplying the dragon's organs with life through miles of arterial cabling.

Finishing their food, they wandered over to one of the giant oil drums which served as a trash can. It stood back from the park's main thoroughfare, at the entrance to one of the shadowy aisles. The passageway was nothing more than a cleft between The Haunted House and a large tented stall offering people bets on mechanical horses racing around a table-top racetrack.

As he dropped his balled up wrapper into the oil drum's murky depths, Jordan thought that he heard the sound of a woman singing. It was only for the briefest of moments, a voice being carried on the gentle breeze, drifting from the night-black crevice. Jordan stood still, straining to hear the voice over the cacophony of sound surrounding him.

Steve walked up next to him. "What are...?"

"Sssh." Jordan held his hand up, signalling for Steve to be quiet. He took a small step towards the dark tunnel-like opening. He leant his head forward, focusing his hearing while peering into the darkness.

After waiting patiently for almost thirty seconds, Steve began again. "What the hell are you doing?" He, too, was staring into the lightless void, with no idea what he was looking for.

"I thought I heard a woman singing." Jordan realised as soon as the words left his mouth how ridiculous this sounded.

"It's called music. They play it through loud speakers." Steve laughed as he pointed up at the speakers silhouetted against the night sky.

"No. Not that singing. It was more like birdsong, but definitely a woman's voice." Jordan took a tentative step towards the black cavity in the fluorescing wall of light.

There it was again. A light, high-pitched song that danced briefly on the wind before dying away, drowned out by the raw maelstrom of rock music being pumped through the chain of crackling speakers. Jordan tilted his head, trying to isolate the sound, but the thumping background beat devoured it, leaving nothing to tell Jordan from where it had emanated, or whom it had come from?

"Did you hear it, just now?" Jordan looked at his friend, a toothy grin spread across his face. "I think it came from there." He pointed into the shadows.

"I didn't hear anything, and I'm sure as hell not following you in there." Steve said, turning away. He was studying the aerodynamic properties of the coconut shy's wooden balls.

Without another word, Jordan took a step forward. As the darkness engulfed, him he felt cooler air on his face. He stood still, allowing his eyes to adjust to the darkness. From behind him he heard Steve mutter, "Oh man. Why did you do that?"

Jordan looked back over his shoulder. Steve was standing in the light, staring towards the spot where his friend had disappeared.

"Where are you?" Steve started creeping towards the thin veil that separated the light and the dark. Just as he was about to cross into the shadows, a face appeared in front of him.

"Boo!" Jordan laughed as his friend screamed out loud in surprise. He quickly darted back into the shadows as Steve, one hand clutching his chest, raised a clenched fist in a mock threat.

As Jordan stepped backwards he felt something tug on the back of his legs. The pressure increased, his weight toppling over until he rocked onto his heels. Something snagged at the crook of his left knee. He briefly felt a sharp burning sensation as he tried in vain to regain his balance. Jordan felt his legs pulled from under him, and for the moment between breaths he floated in space, staring up at the small slit of sky hemmed in by the canvas walls. The neon-bright lights of the funfair obscured the stars. It provided the only reference point Jordan had as he tumbled backwards, arms flailing wildly.

A strangled cry escaped his throat, the air driven from his lungs by the impact of thudding onto the soft grass. He lay still then, surprised and stunned by the assault. Expecting to be robbed or attacked again, he frantically attempted to draw air back into his burning lungs. Shortly afterwards he heard someone approaching and a dark shadow loomed over him. The figure emitted a low rasping laugh. Hands fumbled over his clothing. In a panic, Jordan pushed them away, frantically trying to sit up.

"I'm trying to help you up, you idiot!" Steve's voice emerged from the dark shadow. "You fell over one of the tent's guy ropes. All I saw was you disappearing into the blackness, your hands waving in the air. Then I heard you cry out, so I thought I'd better rescue you." Steve laughed again, although this time, his voice sounded lighter.

With Steve's help, Jordan scrambled back to his feet. "I only cried out because I hit the ground, not because I was scared." Jordan gently rubbed the back of his leg as he spoke.

"Whatever, Dude." Steve tone was both sarcastic and dismissive. Jordan raised his middle finger and gesticulated in Steve's direction. "I don't have to see you to know what you're doing." The two young men laughed in unison.

"Are you okay?" Steve's eyes were beginning to adjust to the darkness. He could make out the vague outline of Jordan, still busy rubbing the back of his knee.

"I've got rope burn. The rope caught behind my knee as I fell. Otherwise I'm fine and dandy." Jordan looked back towards the inviting lights of the main thoroughfare. It was barely ten feet away. "Come on. Let's get outta here."

"What about your mysterious singing woman?" Steve said, peering deeper into the shadowy abyss. "As we have already crossed over and embraced the darkness, we might as well continue our quest." Steve had lowered the tone of his voice and added a nasal twang.

"What was that?" Jordan laughed at his friend.

"Vincent Price." Steve shuffled farther into the darkness, his hand outstretched in front of him.

"It really wasn't." Jordan continued to giggle as he cautiously followed his friend down the claustrophobic passage.

The two youths inched their way through the darkness. Steve used his arm in the same way a blind man used a stick, slowly sweeping the air in front of them before shuffling a forward, a few feet at a time. Jordan's shoes scraped the cracked dry ground under his feet. The grass was long, straw-like. It rustled against their legs as they edged their way through the passage.

Without warning, Steve halted. Barely able to make his friend out in the surrounding gloom, Jordan walked straight into Steve's back. He was just about to complain when Steve took a half step to the side. His voice was no more than a whisper, "Look!" He pointed.

In front of them Jordan could see a small clearing. It was enclosed by the high featureless backdrops of various rides and stalls forming an irregular circle. A halo of neon glow sat above the clearing's high sides, partially brightening the space. The kaleidoscope of colours cast eerie shadows that appeared and disappeared, twisted and contorted onto the taught canvas and wooden wall planks.

A strange void rose from the centre of the clearing. It was blacker than night itself and, unlike the surrounding canvas backdrops, failed to reflect any of the dancing lights and prancing shadows. The shape was similar to an oversize tepee, its wide base funnelling upward into the night sky to form a point. Jordan guessed that it was close to thirty feet high.

Jordan looked at his companion. He could not make out individual facial features, but could sense his friend's apprehension.

"What is it?" He whispered the words, but they still seemed loud in the still air. The clearing was strangely, eerily quiet, Jordan could hear the muffled sounds of the surrounding amusements, but they sounded distant, despite being only a few swift strides away.

"How the fuck should I know?" Steve whispered back, breaking the brief silence. There was no anger in his voice, although Jordan sensed his annoyance at having to answer such a stupid question. It was obvious Steve had no more insight into the mystery than he did. Jordan decided that answering his friends question would only add to Steve's annoyance.

The two boys stood still, cloaked in silence. The dark void remained motionless in the centre of the clearing. Jordan glanced around, but couldn't see anyone else standing there with them. It was a strange oasis of calm, a stark contrast to the surrounding raucous razzamatazz of the fairground. He noticed that, despite its size, when he looked away the void vanished. It simply faded into the background, merging with its surroundings.

A full minute passed, during which both Steve and Jordan considered running back to the known familiarity of the thoroughfare, although neither of them wanted to articulate their fears out loud. When he did finally speak, Steve's voice sounded strange. "Maybe this is responsible for what you heard?"

"I don't think so. It was definitely a woman's voice. Anyway this hasn't made a sound since we've been here." Jordan replied. Bolstered by the sound of his companion's voice, he began to walk towards the pitch-black shadow towering high above him.

As he crept forward, Jordan was aware of the thumping of his heart. It pounded on his ribcage as if trying to escape, not wanting any part of his brain's crazy idea to investigate the anomaly. With each step, he felt his chest constrict. He paused and took a deep breath, filling his lungs with the cool night air. He ran his tongue around the inside of his dry mouth. Not daring to see if Steve was still behind him, he took another step forward.

The shadow began to solidify, taking shape and substance with each of Jordan's hesitant steps. A gentle breeze blew across his face. The black substance rippled and he heard a creaking rustling sound, like the wind blowing through the treetops.

"Oh man, I must need my head examining, following you in here." Steve's voice came from just behind Jordan, who breathed a sigh of relief. His friend had not deserted him.

So Jordan kept walking, his eyes fixed on the shape looming before him. As he got closer, he stretched out his hand. His fingers brushed across a course material. Jordan felt his fingernails snag in the rough surface, which crumbled slightly under his touch. "This feels strange. It's like hessian or canvas, but the top layer is flaky."

As he spoke, a faint light appeared within the structure. The heavy, dark material obscured much of the brightness, but there was no doubt a light had come on inside the shadowy shape. The two young men took a step back, relieved the towering shadow appeared to be nothing more than a large tent, albeit one made from some kind of unusual material. As they stood in the dark, trying to peer into the tent's interior, they both heard a woman's voice singing in a lilting tone that danced through the night air.

"You can hear that, right?" Jordan said looking at his friend's indistinct form.

"Yes I can. We need to get inside and see who it is that has such an awesome voice." Steve began to scrabble excitedly around the base of the tent. Away to Jordan's left, a shaft of light pieced the darkness. He could see the figure of a woman limned by the light. She was evidently holding back the tent flap.

The light from the tent's interior bathed half of the woman's features in pale orange light, the other half remained shrouded in obscurity. Even so, her appearance mesmerised Jordan. When she spoke, her voice was clear and light, each syllable a separate note in the music of her speech.

"Welcome. I am glad that you have found your way to our little show." Jordan detected a slight accent in her voice; eastern European, but he couldn't be sure.

Jordan sensed Steve standing next to him. He glanced at his friend. The light from the tent cast an orange glow onto Steve's face. He was staring at the woman, his mouth hanging open. "So subtle…" Jordan said, shaking his head.

The woman spoke again. "Step inside to witness an aerial display the like of which you have never before seen, and will certainly never see again." Her speech was slow and deliberate. Taking a step to one side she indicated with a flourish of her arm that they should enter the tent.

Steve began to walk towards the tent's opening: instinctively, Jordan grabbed him, pulling him back. Turning his back on the woman, who remained standing patiently in the half-light, Jordan stood in front of his friend. "This is weird. If this is such a great sideshow, why's it hidden in the darkness? Why's it not on the main thoroughfare, where everyone can see it? We've spent most of our lives hanging around The Lair and I've never seen this attraction before… Have you?"

"Not that I can remember, but that doesn't mean it hasn't been here." Steve looked thoughtful, dredging through his memory.

Jordan had whispered his concerns to his friend, convinced the woman had not overheard the conversation. Yet when she spoke, it was to answer his questions. "People are lured… Sorry, that is not the right word." The woman laughed softy, as if enjoying a private joke. "People feel drawn to our show by their own curiosity. Did you not yourselves feel compelled to discover the source of the singing? We do not need a pitch in the bright lights, selling promises and lies, fear and comfort, with equal abandon. Just because you have not seen us does not mean we have not seen you." With that she stepped into the orange shaft of light escaping through the open tent flap.

The two young men could now see the woman clearly for the first time. She was tall and slender. Her long legs were encased in knee-high leather boots with at least six inch high heels. She wore a short dress that glinted and sparkled in the light. Neither boy was sure whether it was black,

95

blue or even green, but they were sure they liked the way it hugged her curves.

Just before she disappeared into the tent's interior she turned her head slightly. Her hair shimmered and blended with her dress, rendering it impossible to tell where one finished and the other began. Her sharp, angular features caught the light and, for a brief moment, Jordan found himself staring into her smouldering brown eyes.

Then she was gone.

Jordan could feel the desire burning within his heart. With the merest of brief glimpses he had been captivated; ensnared by her beauty, enthralled by her inscrutability.

He had to follow her.

Steve's voice came from behind him, breaking into his thoughts. "My god, she has *so* got the hots for you. I take it we are going in?"

"I think that, having come this far, it would be extremely bad manners to just leave without at least watching the show." Jordan smiled, walking towards the tent's open flaps.

"I hope she's got a friend," Steve muttered under his breath as he sauntered after Jordan.

Jordan pushed the flap aside and entered the tent. The material felt rough and prickly, creaking as it moved. He quickly studied the inside wall of the flap. It turned out the material was a thick weave of dry grass and twigs, with an occasional strand of artificial fibre.

The orange light that cast such a strange glow came from four large lanterns mounted on tall, thin pillars in the centre of the tent. The lanterns were weathered brass and looked antique. Jordan took a few steps into the light, his feet sinking into the sand-covered floor.

The young woman stood between the pillars in the middle of the tent. For the first time, Jordan could see her features clearly.

He wasn't disappointed. She was beautiful. The pool of warm light bathing her made her appear almost angelic. As Jordan approached with Steve following closely in his wake, she looked up. The two teenagers tilted their heads back, following her gaze, and looked up into the space above their heads.

High above them, on the edge of shadows, they could see a large trapeze swinging gently back and forth. It was suspended on slender cables hanging from the tent's peak. Perched on the thin pole between them was another woman. As far as Jordan could make out, she wore exactly the same heeled boots and short dress as her companion. And yet she stood on that swinging trapeze with no visible means of support. Her left hand held one of the cables, while with her right she blew a kiss and waved at the boys. Her light giggle echoed softly around the tent.

"Bingo!" Steve said the word quietly, drawing the second syllable out until it died in his throat.

"It's Showtime!" the first woman spoke again, drawing their attention. She beckoned them towards her with long, sylphlike fingers. As they approached her, Jordan was aware of a shadow passing around the walls. Momentarily distracted, he glanced around the tent. When his gaze focused back on their host, she was not alone. Standing next to her was the trapeze woman.

Steve let out a soft whistle. The second woman, now standing in the light, was almost a mirror image of the first. She was taller by a couple of inches. Her dress shorter, but again, only by a few inches. Her hair, parted differently, was identical in colour and length, and, like her twin, it too merged with the scintillating material of her dress.

"O...M...G..." Steve's hoarse whisper hung in the air as the two young men stared into the deep brown eyes of the women standing before them.

"Twins" Even Jordan wasn't sure if this was a question or a simple factual statement.

"That's a common misconception," the women said in unison, before breaking into peals of laughter.

"But you look identical, you even dress the same." Jordan said, aware that he was staring, but completely unable to tear his eyes away.

The first woman smiled at them, an expression of amused pity on her face. "We may look the same to you, but, I can assure you, we are not even related. As for our clothing..." She broke off, looked down at her dress, then over at her companions. "Mine is black with a blue-green hue, whereas hers is clearly black with a green-blue hue."

The two women walked towards the teens, their high-heeled boots barely disturbing the sandy floor as they walked around behind them. Jordan felt the faintest stir of warm breath against the back of his neck. The tiny hairs stood on end as a shiver passed down his spine.

Then, with chirps of delight, the two women were gone. Jordan, following the sound of bird-like laughter, looked up. By the flickering of the orange lantern light he saw the two women swinging on the trapeze. Then, in one smooth movement, they were airborne.

The two women flew in a circle, following the tent's perimeter. They were side by side, arms outstretched, hair trailing behind them. They gradually accelerated with each circuit until they were a just a ghostly blur.

Jordan guessed they must be in some sort of a harness, attached to a cable hanging from the apex of the tent. Not that he could see either the harness or the cable. But then again, would the show be so spectacular if he could?

Then, without warning, the two women abruptly changed direction. With a raucous screech they swooped down towards the young men. Jordan and Steve ducked as the black figures shot overhead, missing them by inches. Jordan looked up just in time to see both women soar into the darkness above.

After a few moments, Jordan heard singing, in a language that neither of the two young men recognised. The refrain was light, the rhythm soothing and hypnotic, like a lullaby.

Jordan and Steve could do nothing apart from stand and stare into the cavernous space above their heads. Abruptly, the lanterns went out.

A thick darkness enveloped them. Jordan swung round instinctively looking to where he guessed the lanterns were. The darkness was total: he was effectively blind.

To his left, he heard a noise like a sheet, hung out to dry, flapping in the breeze, only softer. He felt a gentle breeze brush across his face and ruffle his hair.

Steve cried out. It was a cry born of surprise rather than pain. Then the flapping noise again, only harsher this time, more agitated, the breeze buffeting Jordan's face.

Steve's voice came from further away. "What? Wait…No!" Jordan span around, arms outstretched. He tried to fix on his friends voice, but it was moving, circling in the black void above his head.

Dizzy and disorientated by the darkness, Jordan stumbled over. He fell heavily on his butt, jarring his spine. He flopped over in pain and lay on his back in the cool sand. He could hear the women's shrill laughter cascading down from the darkness.

Suddenly it changed. No more the joyful laughter of young women. It had metamorphosed into the shrieking, screeching caw of a bird of prey in full flight.

Steve's scream filled the air. There was no mistaking the terror in his voice. There was a second scream, joining with the women's unnatural shrieking in a cacophonic bedlam of noise. A sickening thud and a loud crack heralded an eerie hush. The only sound that reached Jordan's ears was that of the amusement park, but it was faint and distant.

Jordan tried to move his legs, but they felt heavy and numb like they belonged to someone else, someone old and decrepit. He called out into the darkness that surrounded him, "Steve, are you there? I'm hurt. I need help."

Then the lanterns flared back into life, bathing the area with orange luminescence. Jordan found himself looking at the woven black tent wall. He turned his head towards the lights. The two women stood between the pillars that supported the lanterns. The light cast shadows across their faces, making them look strangely grotesque. Not that Jordan noticed. His attention was focused on Steve.

His friend lay on his stomach in the sand a few feet away. Steve's hideously twisted neck meant that his face looked up to the roof, his lifeless eyes wide and staring. His mouth had been bleeding and a small pool of blood had formed in the sand next to his ear. The Guns N Roses T-shirt was now ripped and torn, as were his black denim jeans. Through one of the larger holes in the shirt, Jordan saw deep, ugly scratches in Steve's flesh.

Jordan tried to reach out and touch his friend, but his hand fell agonizingly short. He flexed his fingers in the fine sand, desperate to bridge the final few inches.

"Steve." Jordan didn't phrase it as a question, he knew he would never get an answer. Instead, he whispered the word as an apologetic farewell.

A pair of huge talons alighted in the space between him and Steve's broken body, obscuring his line of sight. He could feel tears forming in the corners of his eyes. He didn't know what had inspired them; was it Steve's demise, his pain, or his own frustration and fear?

He looked up through the tears. Briefly, he mistook the figure standing over him to be an angel. He saw the giant wings, spread wide, blocking the light. Black feathers shone like polished jet, the reflected lantern light lending them a flaming orange aura.

Then the beast let out an ear-splitting shriek, lifting one of its feet. The mighty talons hovered above Jordan. He lay still, paralysed by fear. Resigned to his fate, he awaited the coup de grace.

Jordan liked to believe that when his time came he'd be brave and stare death in the face. He felt an embarrassing mix of fear and shame as he closes his eyes. He expected the razor-sharp talons to carve his flesh from the bone.

But the strike never comes. Instead he felt their powerful grip on the waistband of his jeans. A sudden rustle of the giant wings and Jordan was airborne. He could feel the breeze on his body as he is propelled through the air. His limbs hung limply, their weight applying pressure to his back, ramping up the pain.

Then the temperature changed, the warm, stuffy heat of the tent replaced by the cool, fresh air of the night. He could feel the shuddering, rhythmic thump of the beast's wings as they ascended into the night sky.

Jordan tentatively opened his eyes. Above him, the black shape of the beast silhouetted against the silvery blue canopy of the night. Twisting his head, he looked down at the amusement park far below. He could hear the distant sound of people enjoying themselves, then even that faded as they left the park behind. They were soon flying high above Dragon Back's main street. The town appeared almost deserted at this late hour.

They left the town behind and began circling above the dark, sinister cliffs. The beast appeared to be waiting, riding the up draft to gain height, then gliding back down in long, lazy arcs.

Jordan heard the second beast shrieking and he sensed their wait was over. He struggled to look in the direction from which the sound came. The second beast was flying towards them, Steve's limp body hanging from its massive talons. As it got closer, the beast holding him let out a shrill screech and let go of his jeans.

Jordan cried out, fear gripping him as he tumbled through the air. He flailed his arms, as if hoping he had suddenly developed the ability to fly. Then he was hit hard as the second beast slammed into him, catching him in mid-air. He screamed in pain as the shock of the impact shook his body. He was hanging upside down, talons gripping his thigh. Below he saw the waves breaking over the rocks at the foot of the cliffs.

Jordan tried not to look at his dead friend's battered body far below him. The beast was hovering just above the cliff top. Jordan could see the inverted image of the first young woman perched on the jagged crags at the cliff's edge.

"I told you the show was like nothing you had ever seen before." She giggled, her hand brushing the hair away from her face. Then she added, "Or will again." She blew Jordan a kiss.

The beast released his leg. As Jordan plunged headfirst towards the serrated, black rocks below, his last thought before his body smashed against their unforgiving sharpness was one of realisation. He knew now where Dragon Back's sinister reputation had really come from...

Recreational Killing

I can't tell you my name. Not because it's a secret, but because I don't know it. Well, I do — I just can't remember it. That's the weird thing about the human brain; you can damage it and never know. Emotional damage leaves no physical wound a doctor can suture; no scar you can point to and say, "That hurt." But the pain's still there, festering deep in the convoluted folds of your mind, gradually spreading from neuron to neuron, until one day you are no longer you.

Then you snap.

I snapped. I don't mean I rebelled against society's petty rules, the social norms we accept as nasty but necessary. I mean totally fucking snapped — burnt my house down because it contained too many memories and just walked away. I didn't have a clue where I was going. By disassociating myself from society I no longer felt bound by convention or restrained by etiquette. I was ready to unleash my pent-up guilt, pain and anger on the first person who dared to confront me.

That poor unfortunate soul turned out to be a rookie police officer. He was responding to an intruder call, and disturbing my breakfast in the process. I had thought the house empty; there was no car and the house had remained dark throughout the evening. So I let myself in through the kitchen window. But, unbeknown to me, there was a woman sleeping upstairs. She, on hearing the glass smash, phoned the police, who, to their credit, responded immediately. Had the young officer not been so keen, deciding, instead, to finish his donut and coffee, I'm reasonably sure he would be alive today. The homeowner almost certainly would.

If curiosity killed the cat then it was naivety which slaughtered the cop. Walking up to the front door and ringing the bell is simply asking to be killed. Opening the door, I plunged the kitchen knife into his throat. He didn't have time to speak before I slammed the door shut, leaving him bleeding to death on the white stone step.

The woman was even easier. She'd simply walked down the stairs and into the kitchen before realising I was standing there. I think the penny dropped a split-second before her own carving knife ripped through her soft, bloated double chin. I stepped over her still twitching body and got my breakfast 'to go,' before calmly walking out of the back door.

Now, even though I might've been experiencing a psychotic break, I knew what I'd done was wrong — I just didn't care. In fact I was enjoying it. It was an exciting excursion on my sabbatical from reality. I wanted to go again, wanted to experience that moment of supreme power over and over. That split-second where they know, without a shadow of doubt, they are looking into the face of death.

So I started running.

I ran until my legs could no longer hold me up and my stomach spewed blood, then I ran some more. That was about six months ago, judging by the changing seasons, but, as I'm no longer a slave to the passage of time and have no use for calendars or clocks, I can't be sure. But I'm still running and yes, I'm still killing.

The sound of a vehicle, the driver grinding its gears as they navigate the twisty incline, wakes me from my slumbers. I'd taken shelter in an old mining hut, its presence long ago obscured from the road by an overabundance of vegetation. The original access to the little shack was by a steep track from the road, winding its way up the mountainside which had long since been closed to the public for safety reasons, allowing nature to reclaim the track as forestland.

The hut, one of several scattered across this area I used for shelter, overlooked a small lake with an overnight stop-off point located on its opposite shore; it's from there the engine noise emanates. An excessively large recreational vehicle had slowly driven into the clearing, rocking back and forth as it bounced across the uneven ground. Its sheer size making it cumbersome and awkward as it weaved between the tall pines, finally coming to a halt with one last crunching gear change.

I'd left the secluded hut immediately the noise alerted me to the RV's presence. Six months surviving in the wilderness had taught me to sleep light and move fast, so I hid in the tree line, a few yards back from the water's edge, on my side of the lake. The driver killed the engine, a brief moment of surreal peace followed during which I stared across the water at the giant interloper, its shiny chrome headlights staring defiantly back. A side door burst open, disgorging a young woman. She sprinted across the dusty surface towards the lake. A man of similar age followed her, trying to grab her as she ran into the water, where finally he caught her with a flying tackle, sending both of them tumbling headfirst into the cold lake.

I watched the young couple surface, the woman angrily pushing the lad away. He tried splashing her playfully while they stood waist deep in the water, but I clearly heard her say, "Fuck off!" as she headed back to the shore. I'd been so focused on their dash to the lake and subsequent argument the sound of another voice surprised me.

"When you two have finished we have to set up for the night." The voice belonged to a woman who, from my vantage point, looked to be a thirty year older version of the young woman wading out of the lake. Both were blond, although the younger woman's hair appeared brighter and more vibrant; I guessed it was her natural colouring whereas the older one bleached out the encroaching greyness of age. She is also thin and sinewy with a dark tan making her look like a scrawny Barbie doll, whereas the younger woman was more curvaceous, with some gentle muscle tone adding definition to her paler skin.

While the women, who I assumed were mother and daughter, returned to the RV the man wrung out his wet T-shirt. He had the long scruffy hair and well-built, if a little skinny, body you would expect to see in a surfer scene on Hawaii-Five O. I watched from my vantage point as he unzipped before letting loose a stream of urine into the glass-like pool.

The older of the two women appeared in the vehicle's open doorway and shouted for him to help. He zipped up and strolled back to the door, there he collected a collapsible table and some fold up chairs, which he set up with little enthusiasm. After a few minutes I smelt the tantalising aroma of bacon wafting on the light evening breeze.

Remaining hidden, I watched this encroachment of civilisation into my territory, acutely aware I haven't seen the other person who must surely be there. The older blonde needed a husband, the daughter a father. He must still be inside the RV, maybe resting after the day's drive while the women prepare supper. I also found myself pondering surfer dude's position in this perfect little family.

He was probably the young girl's boyfriend, but the older woman doesn't appear to hold him in much esteem. Perhaps she doesn't think him good enough for her daughter; on first impressions I had to agree. He appeared lazy and self-indulgent. I'd be doing them a favour by killing him. Okay, so I'm going to kill them too, but I could do him first.

As I watched, the girl brought out some plastic plates and sets the small table with four place settings. The youth grabbed her around the waist again, in an effort to pull her onto his lap, but she told him off angrily as she wriggled free before stomping back to the RV. He gave a resigned shrug, but remained staring out across the lake, his eyes fixed on my position. Despite having carefully hidden myself below a large weeping willow, its branches overhanging the pond, tickling the water's surface, I tensed up, ready to run. Had he seen me?

I remained perfectly still, staring back at the gangly youth, waiting for him to shout, to point in my direction, alerting the family to my presence. But he remains seated, his gaze moving to the other side of the lake as the pretty girl returned with plastic mugs and picnic cutlery.

He reluctantly helped lay the table and I relaxed a little, the adrenaline coursing through my veins begins to fade, leaving me feeling flushed and shaky. I loosed the grip on my hunting knife, not knowing at what point I'd considered it necessary to reach for it; my forearm felt tense and sore. I flexed my fingers, encouraging the blood to flow right to their tips. Across the still water, the young woman collects plates of food through an open window before carrying them to the table.

Then I saw him. He stood in the doorway of the RV looking out towards the picnic table. At first glance you wouldn't have noticed him. Not because he was standing in a shadowy doorway or looking to blend in to his surroundings, but because he possessed the most nondescript appearance imaginable. He was neither fat nor thin, and while he couldn't be described as tall, he wasn't short either, and dressed in shapeless grey joggers with a black, maybe dark blue sweatshirt, your eyes would just pass him over. Instantly forgettable — *he would make the perfect spy*, I thought with a smirk.

He hovered briefly in the doorway, as if weighing up whether to leave the sanctuary of the vehicle or not, but eventually he walked slowly down the steps and out into the evening sun. He looked older than the Barbie doll woman and I thought at first he might be her father, but the way they kissed quickly dispelled that thought.

The middle-aged man strolled to the makeshift alfresco diner, but from my distant vantage point appeared reluctant to join the younger couple, who were now sitting at either end of the table, pointedly ignoring each other. Relationships among the family looked to be strained. I wondered if it was a result of travelling together, cooped up in that glorified caravan, or did it run deeper, some fundamental flaw in the family dynamic.

I sat watching them eat, starkly aware of how hungry I was. I hadn't eaten properly for a few days, or was it longer? I'd stolen a few supplies from a group of rock climbers and then killed a rabbit. I would've killed the climbers too, but they were young, athletic and they outnumbered me. I might not be all there up top, but I'm not fucking stupid. This family however, well they were ripe for the taking.

Settling back, I waited for darkness to fall.

In this part of the mountains the sun sets early, dipping behind the higher western ridges; the waning moon's reflected light too weak to pierce the forest's canopy, therefore leaving the campsite in near total darkness. I watched as they tidied away their meal, the women going inside to wash up while the older man sat with his feet on the picnic table, drinking a beer Barbie Doll had brought him. Surfer dude sat with him in silence for a few minutes, then, evidently bored, sauntered down to the water's edge to skim pebbles across the lake.

The interior RV lights gradually shine brighter as darkness started to wrap itself around the lake. The older man finished his beer, going inside only to re-emerge with a couple of lanterns, the modern type which glowed without really brightening their surroundings. He put them on the ground before disappearing back inside.

I decided the time was right to move closer. From where they were they wouldn't be able to see me skirting the edge of the lake, providing I kept low and quiet. Surfer dude had given up skimming stones and was smoking a joint he'd retrieved from the RV. As I got closer I smelt its flowery sweetness drifting across the clearing as he perched on the RV's oversized front fender.

I crept round to the back edge of the campsite and took up a new position in the deep darkness of the forest, well away from the more open and slightly lighter lake. Crouching down, I prepared to wait for my opportunity, hoping they would soon retire to bed, tired from the day's journey. Through the open door I could hear music playing, country and western mostly, occasionally accompanied by the loud and out of tune voice of the father-figure. During a particularly bad rendition of *'Islands in the Stream'* I saw him through one of the windows, dancing with Barbie Doll. It reminded me of before the accident, when I had a family, watching those terrible reality programmes on Saturday nights. It wouldn't matter how bad they would get you just couldn't tear yourself away.

I must have nodded off, because I was suddenly awoken by a commotion from the doorway of the family's camper. The man I thought was her father, was pushing the young girl out into the darkness. She's putting up a fight, clutching at the sides of the doorway, her feet scrabbling for purchase on the loose surface. She screamed at him to let her stay, that she didn't like the dark; that she'd be quiet. Tears streamed down her cheeks, the ruined mascara, coupled with the eerie yellow glow from the lanterns, casting her face with an ugly clown-like appearance.

The man's foot pressed into her chest — it must have squashed her breast because she yells in pain, letting go of the doorway to clutch at his foot. In that instant his knee straightened, sending the young woman tumbling backwards. She sat hunched on the ground holding her chest and fighting to stem the flow of tears. She was clearly struggling to draw breath, but neither Barbie Mum nor Surfer Dude lifted a finger to help. Before she had a chance to get to her feet a bundle of clothes and what looked like a sleeping bag, land in the dirt next to her, after which the door slammed shut.

The young man, having chosen to sleep outside had already unrolled his sleeping bag, laughed at her. "Are you scared? Afraid something horrible is lurking in the woods ready to gobble you all up?" I can't see his face, but the tone of his voice told me he was sneering.

"I'm not scared. I just don't like the dark," the young woman snivelled as she climbed to her feet and gathered her belongings.

"Maybe I'll come over later. Who knows, you might even enjoy it?" The young man wasn't laughing now, his voice taking on a sinister tone.

"Fuck off, you creep." The woman moved to the other end of the RV, as far away from the man as the clearing and lantern light would allow. She sat down, almost within touching distance of where I lay, concealed in the shadowy undergrowth. If I just reached out my hand...

But I didn't.

I didn't want to be discovered now and lose the element of surprise. Besides, this was going to be fun. So instead I laid still while the girl set out her blanket and sleeping bag, barely five feet away.

The surfer dude sat smoking for a while. He was no more than a patch of shadow in the surrounding darkness until he pulled on his tote, the flaring joint grotesquely illuminating his features. He showed no more interest in the girl. She lay with her back arching away from me, having tightly wrapped herself in the protective cocoon of the sleeping bag. I could just about hear her rhythmic breathing above the background noise of woodland critters, but I doubted she was asleep, not with his chilling suggestion hanging over her.

After a while the young man relieved himself again then, sitting on his bedroll, removed his jeans and cloaked himself in a rug before settling down to sleep. "Don't you be coming over here to steal a look at my cock, Sara. I know you want to," his voice came from the darkness. A barely audible groan from her prone form followed his words. Again, I heard his laughter carrying on the breeze from across the clearing.

I waited quietly in the bushes for another half hour, hoping they were asleep, before cautiously sliding from my hiding place. I crept around the clearing's edge, keeping away from the light until I'd rounded the rear of the RV, putting it between me and the two young people lying out under the stars. As I drew closer to the caravan's sleeper section, I heard muffled movements from within. I tip-toed closer, keeping my head down to avoid being seen through one of the three small windows evenly spaced along its length.

I knelt quietly below the middle window, listening for sounds of discovery. The older man is talking, his gruff voice raised, excited, his words hurried and garbled. Then I hear a female's excited moan. The unmistakable groan of ecstatic pleasure, making me realise why Sara wasn't permitted to spend the night in the caravan. Barbie mama and her man were getting it on.

Carefully raising my head I peered through the window and saw them together on the narrow bed in the rear quarter of the caravan. His pale bloated body was thrusting frantically, her twiglet-like legs sticking out on either side of his bare ass. As I watched, the man lets out a loud groan before collapsing across his lover. The two of them lay entwined, panting heavily as I duck back out of sight, making my way down the side of the RV.

I edged quietly towards the front of the mobile home, making my way to the driver's cab, and the door. I'm now sure there are only four of them; Barbie and the old man, both inside the caravan and sure to doze off soon, and surfer dude and the daughter, Sara. The latter two were outside and likely to be the most troublesome. Although the young man had been mixing alcohol and weed throughout the evening, he was still well-built and muscular, while Sara, although probably not as strong, looked athletic and certainly appeared to own a feisty temperament.

I placed my hand on the door handle, giving it a gentle tug. The spring mechanism opened, the soft click sounded loud in the still night air and the interior light shone like a beacon. I froze, my hand on the plastic handle and the door barely open an inch, listening for any sound to indicate I'd been heard. From the rear of the caravan I heard Barbie giggle and a door slamming shut, leaving me with the deafening silence of night.

I gently teased the door open until the gap was wide enough for me to climb inside. I flicked the interior light off and carefully pulled the door closed without actually shutting it, doing so would undoubtedly make too much noise and probably cause the vehicle to rock. I wanted to preserve my precious advantage of surprise for as long as I could. A few weeks ago I'd killed six campers, as they were searching for firewood and erecting their tents, without being detected. The last person to die, a man of about eighty with a weathered face and deep tan, was as astonished as the young man trying to get a phone signal. He'd died first; stupid thing to do, wandering off alone into the wilderness.

It had become a game to me, not to mention a matter of pride; spree killing without detection. A cross between *What's the Time Mr Wolf* and *Cluedo*. My victims fit no discernible pattern; creed, colour, sex, age, it made no difference. I didn't even have a modus operandi: I just slaughtered indiscriminately. No motive, with the occasional exception of needing food, all I needed was opportunity. Cross my path and I'd kill you. Just for kicks.

I quickly checked the ignition and, finding no keys, widened my search to the dash and central console. Still nothing. They were probably in Daddy's pocket, but at least I knew they weren't prepared for a quick getaway. I slid from the driver's chair and skipped lightly across the thick nylon carpet to the small kitchen area. A swift glance down the caravan's central corridor told me Barbie was still lying on the bed, her fake-tanned body clearly visible through the open door. She had made no effort to cover up and was face down on the pale rumpled sheets as if asleep.

The compact toilet is almost opposite me, the door firmly shut, the little red indicator telling me it's *occupied*. I heard movement from inside, then the sound of the toilet flushing. I quietly removed my hunting knife from its soft scabbard, and waited my chance. The lock flicked to *vacant* and the flimsy door swung open.

I darted behind it, weapon poised.

The floor creaked as the family's patriarch stepped out of the bathroom, his fingers wrapped around the edge of the door, ready to swing it shut.

I draw back my elbow. The shiny blade glimmered in the half-light, my arm waiting patiently.

The door swung closed and I came face to face with Barbie's lover. His mouth gaped open as he looked into my face — I've not shaved for months, my beard and hair hanging in long tangled strands — but before he could speak, or scream, or anything else, I punched him in the mouth. My fist smacked into his lips, crushing them against his teeth, the force of the impact knocking one of his incisors from his mouth, the blade of my knife tore through his flimsy soft palate, fatally spearing his brain stem.

I pulled my arm back, dragging the razor-sharp steel free, and caught his corpse as it sunk into my arms. I looked into his eyes, but they were already dull and lifeless, the pupils blown wide. I stepped back to let the limp body slip soundlessly to the floor, where I left it, and made my way towards the bedroom's open door.

Towards Barbie's sun ravaged nakedness.

Stepping into the room, I noticed she hadn't moved. The quiet rhythmic sound of her breathing told me she's fallen asleep following her earlier bout of love-making. I'm just about to move closer to the bed when I hear the RV's side door swing open. I spin round in time to see Surfer Dude staring at the open-mouthed corpse lying in the narrow corridor. Hearing me move, he turned his head, and the hunting rifle he had grasped in his hands, in my direction.

The first shot was wild and uncontrolled. Surfer Dude stumbling and off balance, the weapon, still moving in his hands as he pulled the trigger. Above me, the skylight exploded, showering the room with tiny orange plastic fragments.

The loud explosion of noise in the cramped caravan awakens Barbie with a start and she sits up. Before she had time to assess what's going on, I grabbed her bleached hair and, dragging her from the bed, pushed her towards Surfer Dude. She stumbled towards him as he raised his gun a second time. Briefly, I saw his face; the confused look of panic.

I didn't just hear the blast, I felt it. Barbie's head disintegrated before my eyes, a thin red spray flying towards me in slow motion. In an instant I'm covered in bright red blood and sticky, grey brain matter, inside my mouth felt crunchy, like eggshell, I spat out several slivers of white skull. Barbie's body, minus its head, lay crumpled at the feet of the young man. He still held the rifle, although with no real conviction, his gaze fixed upon the bloody stump where Barbie's head had once been.

The air stinks of cordite and fresh blood, the smoking barrel giving it a blue tinge. He stood barely seven feet from me, so if I'd thrown myself full-length I would probably knock him over. But the bed's corner jutted between us, blocking the one good stride I needed to take off, to really launch myself with power. I edged slightly to my left, giving myself room and simultaneously closing the gap between us to six feet. But it's still too far. If he stepped back, if I missed the gun, if I fell short, then... bang! I would die. The odds were still in his favour.

I inched left again, Barbie's blood stinging my eyes as I risked a quick downward glance. I now had a clear path around the edge of the bed. The only thing between me and Dude is Barbie's decapitated body. He must've seen me moving because he's roused from the paralysing shock which accompanied blowing a relative's head off. He swung the barrel towards me and levelled it at my chest, tears streaming down his face. He attempted to speak, but his mouth opened and closed with nothing more than a gasping snivel.

Looking at the emotional young man pointing the gun at me, I understood how my nameless victims had felt staring into my face, gasping their last breath. The police officer, the homeowner, the campers, climbers and joggers, even the old man, all knew who their murderer had been. I couldn't take the credit for Barbie, she was Dude's kill. Maybe I could claim an assist? Anyway I'm now the one staring death in the ugly, spotty face, events having turned full circle. Life was like that.

The gunshot sounded like an explosion within the tiny confines of the RV, my eyes closed automatically as I waited for the inevitable horse-like kick to my chest which would throw my mangled torso against the caravan's flimsy wall.

But it never came. I opened my eyes in time to see blood spew from Surfer Dude's mouth as the rifle clattered to the floor. He clutched at the blood-soaked doorframe before sliding to the carpet next to Barbie's headless body. Sara stood motionless behind him, a second hunting rifle smoking in her hand.

I looked at her in disbelief. She's just shot… who, her brother? Or is it her boyfriend? Anyway she did it saving me… her father's killer, and for all she knew, her mother's killer. Wanting to say something, I opened my mouth but the words didn't come. What could you say in these circumstances?

Sara crouched next to the groaning figure of the young man, lifting his head by the hair so she could look into his face. He coughed weakly, spraying tiny droplets of blood across her shirt, before slipping away. She let go of his hair, dropping his head to the floor with a thud, before getting to her feet and turning away, barely stopping to look at Barbie. She paused briefly in the kitchenette to shoot the older man's corpse in the groin, before calmly stepping down from the vehicle.

I followed her out, unsure what to do. What to say. Her gun lay discarded in the dirt while she carried one of the lanterns down to the water's edge. I hung back while she stripped off her blood-splattered shirt and washed herself clean. I couldn't help wondering if the gesture was as much symbolic, a psychological cleansing, as it was physical.

She dried herself with the unsoiled areas of her screwed-up shirt, something my daughter would have done when playing in the blow-up paddling pool in our garden. Before the drunk driver turned our car into twisted metal, and people would cross the street to avoid talking to me. But then, what do you say to a man who had lost his entire family?

I went back inside the RV and rummaged around until I found a suitcase that might belong to a teenage girl. I took out a clean shirt and pulled a towel off the drying rail before going back outside. Sara stood limply by the door as if unsure what to expect. Handing her the towel, I noticed her mouth curving into a half smile, but her eyes remained cold and distant.

I knew that look, the look of disassociation.

One day Sara might tell me why she helped kill her family, but I'm not going to ask. I may, one day, tell her what happened to my family, but only if she asks. I may even tell her my name… if I remember it, because that's what a man does.

And I am a man, a man with a family.

Made in the USA
Charleston, SC
20 February 2015